开心故事

Funny Stories

The Commercial Press

Published by:
The Commercial Press (U.S.) Ltd.
The Corporation, 2nd Floor
New York, NY 10013

Funny Stories
Elementary Readings in Language and Culture

Author: Hong Ziping
Editor: Rachel Feng, Skyle Kwok

ISBN: 978 962 07 1954 7
Printed in Hong Kong

http://www.chinese4fun.net

Contents
目　录

PUBLISHER'S NOTE

After studying one to two years of Chinese you have also gained the knowledge of quite a bit of vocabulary. You may be wondering whether there are any other ways for you to further improve your Chinese language proficiency? Although there are a lot of books in the market that are written for people who are studying Chinese it is not easy to find an interesting and easy to read book that matches up to one's level of proficiency. You may find the content and the choice of words for some books to be too difficult to handle. You may also find some books to be too easy and the content is too naive for high school students and adults. Seeing the demand for this kind of learning materials we have designed a series of reading materials, which are composed of vivid and interesting content, presented in a multi-facet format. We think this can help students who are learning Chinese to solve the above problem. Through our reading series you can improve your Chinese and at the same time you will learn a lot of Chinese culture.

Our series includes Chinese culture, social aspects of China, famous Chinese literary excerpts, pictorial symbols of China, famous Chinese heroes...and many other indispensable aspects of China for those who want to really understand Chinese culture. While enjoying the reading materials one can further one's knowledge of Chinese culture from different angles. The content of the series are contextualized according to the wordbase categorization of The content of the series are contextualized according to the word base categorization of HSK and GCS. We have selected our diction from the elementary, beginner, intermediate to advanced level of Chinese language learners. Our series is suitable for students at the pre-intermediate, intermediate to advanced level of Chinese and working people who are studying Chinese on their own.

The body of our series is composed of literary articles. The terms used in each article are illustrated with the romanised system called Hànyǔ pīnyīn for the ease in learning the pronunciation. Each article has an English translation with explanation of the vocabulary. Moreover there is related background knowledge in Expansion Reading. Interesting games are added to make it fun to learn. We aim at presenting a three-dimensional study experience of learning Chinese for our readers.

Bàba yǔ érzi

爸爸与儿子

Father and Son

Pre-reading Questions

1. What kind of topics do you talk about with your parents?

2. How will you face your parents if you get an unsatisfactory result at school?

Zuòwén fēnshù
❶ 作文 分数

Bàba Érzi shàngxīngqī nǐ yào wǒ xiě de nà
爸爸："儿子，上星期 你 要 我 写 的 那

piān zuòwén lǎoshī gěi de fēnshù gāo ma
篇 作文，老师 给 的 分数 高 吗？"

Érzi Fēnshù hěn
儿子："分数 很

dī a
低 啊。"

Bàba Wèishénme
爸爸："为什么

ne
呢？"

Father is working on the homework with the son.

1

儿子：_{Érzi} "老师_{Lǎoshī} 说_{shuō} 作文_{zuòwén} 的_{de} 内容_{nèiróng} 不_{bù} 适合_{shìhé}。"

爸爸：_{Bàba} "不_{Bù} 会_{huì} 吧_{ba}，不_{bù} 是_{shì}《我_{Wǒ} 的_{de} 爸爸_{bàba}》

吗_{ma}? 我_{Wǒ} 觉得_{juéde} 自己_{zìjǐ} 写_{xiě} 得_{de} 很_{hěn} 好_{hǎo}。"

儿子：_{Érzi} "是_{Shì} 啊_a，可是_{kěshì} 你_{nǐ} 写_{xiě} 的_{de} 是_{shì} 我_{wǒ} 的_{de}

爷爷_{yéye}! "

Translation

❶ Composition Grade

The father says, 'Son, did you get a high grade for the composition you wanted me to write for you last week?'

The son replies, 'I got a low grade.'

The father asks, 'How come?'

The son answers, 'The teacher said the composition doesn't quite fit the assignment

The father says, 'You must be kidding. Isn't the title "My Father"? I think I did a good job.'

The son answers, 'You're right about the title. But you wrote about my grandpa!'

❷ 合着眼
Hé zhe yǎn

儿子 放学 回家 后，
Érzi fàngxué huíjiā hòu

对 爸爸 说：“好 爸爸，
duì bàba shuō Hǎo bàba

你 能够 合 着 眼，在 纸上
nǐ nénggòu hé zhe yǎn zài zhǐshang

写 出 你 的 名字 吗？”
xiě chu nǐ de míngzi ma

爸爸 说：“这 有 什么
Bàba shuō Zhè yǒu shénme

困难 呢？我 合 着 眼 写 几 行 字 也 可以。”
kùnnan ne Wǒ hé zhe yǎn xiě jǐ háng zì yě kěyǐ

儿子 说：“爸爸，不用 你 写 几 行 字 啊。”
Érzi shuō Bàba bùyòng nǐ xiě jǐ háng zì a

儿子 拿出 成绩表，说：“爸爸，你 现在 合
Érzi náchu chéngjìbiǎo shuō Bàba nǐ xiànzài hé

着 眼，在 上面 写上 你 的 名字 就 可以。”
zhe yǎn zài shàngmian xiěshàng nǐ de míngzi jiù kěyǐ

The report of a chinese student

Translation

❷ With Eyes Closed

After coming home from school, the son says to his father, 'Dad, can you write your name on a piece of paper with your eyes closed?'

The father replies, 'It's a piece of cake. I can even write a few lines with my eyes closed.'

The son adds, 'Dad, I don't need you to write a few lines.'

Then, the son holds out his school report card and says, 'Dad, please close your eyes and write your name on this.'

❸ 害怕
Hàipà

爸爸："儿子，考你一道题：树上有
Bàba　　　　Érzi　　kǎo nǐ yī dào tí　shùshang yǒu

两只鸟，打死了一只，还有多少只呢？"
liǎng zhī niǎo　dǎsǐ le yī zhī　　háiyǒu duōshao zhī ne

儿子："一只。"
Érzi　　　Yī zhī

爸爸："不对！另外一只鸟害怕，还不
Bàba　　　Bùduì　Lìngwài yī zhī niǎo hàipà　hái bù

飞走吗？"
fēi zǒu ma

儿子："明白了。"
Érzi　　　Míngbai le

爸爸："再问你一道题，如果回答得
Bàba　　　Zài wèn nǐ yī dào tí　rúguǒ huídá de

不好，晚上没饭吃！"
bù hǎo　wǎnshang méi fàn chī

A Chinese Middle School

4

Érzi　Hǎo　ba
儿子：“好 吧。”

Bàba　Fángzi　lǐmiàn　zhǐyǒu　nǐ　yī　gè　rén　wǒ
爸爸：“房子 里面 只有 你 一 个 人，我

xiànzài　jìnlai　le　yǒu　jǐ　gè　rén
现在 进来 了，有 几 个 人？”

Érzi　Yī　gè
儿子：“一 个。”

Bàba　Zěnme　háishi　yī　gè　ne
爸爸：“怎么 还是 一 个 呢？”

Érzi　Wǒ　hàipà　pǎo　le
儿子：“我 害怕，跑 了。”

Translation

❸ About Fear

The father says, 'Son, let me ask you a question. There were two birds in a tree, but one was shot dead. How many remained?'

The son answers, 'One.'

The father says, 'Wrong! Wouldn't the other bird fly away because it was afraid?'

The son replies, 'I get it.'

The father says, 'I'll ask you another question. If you get the wrong answer, you're not allowed to have dinner!'

The son answers, 'Okay.'

The father says, 'You're the only one in the house. And I just came in. How many people are there in the house?'

The son replies, 'One.'

The father asks, 'Still one? Why?'

The son replies, 'I ran away because I was afraid.'

❹ 从 小时候 做 起

儿子 在 上课 的 时候，经常 跟 旁边 的

同学 说话。

爸爸：“这 是 不 对 的。你 以后 要 改

过来，知道 吗？”

儿子：“爸爸，为什么 要 改 呢？老师 在

上课 的 时候 说 的 话 比 我 多 啊。”

爸爸：“老师 要 教 你们 知识，怎么 能

不 说话 呢？”

儿子：“你 说 过，很 多 事情 要 从

小时候 做 起。我 长大 后 要 当 老师，现在

不 练习 怎么 行？”

Translation

④ Starting from Childhood

The son often talks to his classmates sitting next to him in class.

The father admonishes his son saying, 'What you've been doing is wrong. You've got to stop it now. Is that clear?'

The son answers, 'Dad, why should I stop doing it? The teachers talk much more than I do in class.'

The father answers, 'How can they teach you without talking a lot?'

The son replies, 'You said many things must be practiced starting from childhood. I'm going to be a teacher when I grow up, so I have no choice but to practice talking now.'

Expansion Reading

The Severe Father (严父 , *Yanfu*)

'The mother is kind and the father is severe (慈母严父 , *cimuyanfu*),' as a Chinese saying goes. This means that traditionally the mother is responsible for doing the housework and taking care of the children. She tends to indulge the kids and tolerate their being spoiled and capricious. On the contrary, the father is the head of the family and is responsible for putting bread on the table and disciplining the children. When maintaining discipline, the father is always strict with the children in a serious and severe manner. In the eyes of the children, the father is authoritarian - defying him merits physical punishment.

A Chinese family

In modern Chinese society, although husband and wife share the responsibility of disciplining the kids, the father still bears most of the burden. Many couples still follow the labor division mode of 'the mother is kind and the father is severe (慈母严父).' Under this division of labor however, the modern 'Severe Father (严父 , *yanfu*)' is quite different from the traditional one in that the father is 'strict (严 , *yan*)' mainly in making requirements, not in his attitude towards the children. In many families with one child, both parents tend to be kind and not severe, even to the point of being unduly indulgent, which is considered a common social issue.

GAMES FOR FUN

Below is a riddle about father and son. Can you guess the answer?

Two fathers and two sons go out to buy hats, but only three hats are bought. Why?

Māma   yǔ   háizi
妈妈与孩子
Mother and Children

Pre-reading Questions

1. What are the images of parents from the children's point of view?

2. How do parents usually express their caring?

Zhàogù
❶ 照顾

Yǒu   yī   tiān,   nǚ'ér   tūrán   duì   bàba   shuō
有 一 天 ， 女 儿 突 然 对 爸 爸 说 ：

Bàba   wǒ   kěyǐ   gēn   nǐ   shuō jiàn shì   ma
"爸 爸 ， 我 可 以 跟 你 说 件 事 吗 ？ "

Bàba   shuō   Kěyǐ   a
爸 爸 说 ： "可 以 啊 。 "

Nǚ'ér   xiǎo   shēng   shuō   Bàba   wǒ   juéde   māma   bù
女 儿 小 声 说 ： "爸 爸 ， 我 觉 得 妈 妈 不

huì   zhàogù   xiǎohái
会 照 顾 小 孩 。 "

Bàba   hěn   qíguài   wèn   nǚ'ér   Nǐ   wèishénme   zhèyàng
爸 爸 很 奇 怪 ， 问 女 儿 ： "你 为 什 么 这 样

shuō
说 ？ "

Nǚ'ér shuō Měicì wǒ bù xiǎng shuìjiào de shíhou
女儿 说："每次 我 不 想 睡觉 的 时候，

māma dōu yào wǒ shuìjiào Měicì wǒ hěn xiǎng shuìjiào de
妈妈 都 要 我 睡觉。每次 我 很 想 睡觉 的

shíhou māma yòu yào bǎ wǒ jiào qǐlai
时候，妈妈 又 要 把 我 叫 起来。"

Translation

1 Taking Care of the Children

One day, the daughter says to the father unexpectedly, 'Dad, I have something to talk to you about.'

The father answers, 'Well, I'm listening.'

The daughter whispers, 'Dad, I don't think Mom is good at taking care of kids.'

Feeling curious, the father asks the daughter, 'What makes you think so?'

The daughter replies, 'Whenever I don't want to sleep, Mom always asks me to go to bed. But whenever I feel sleepy, she always gets me out of bed.'

❷ 一句话都没说
<small>Yī jù huà dōu méi shuō</small>

<small>Wǎnfàn hòu   māma gēn mèimei zài xǐ wǎn   bàba gēn</small>
晚饭 后，妈妈 跟 妹妹 在 洗 碗，爸爸 跟

<small>érzi   zài kàn diànshì</small>
儿子 在 看 电视。

<small>Tūrán   chuánlai le dōngxi diào zài dìshang de shēngyīn</small>
突然，传来 了 东西 掉 在 地上 的 声音，

<small>ránhòu biàn zài méiyǒu shēngyīn le</small>
然后 便 再 没有 声音 了。

<small>Érzi   duì   bàba   shuō   Yīdìng shì māma gàn de</small>
儿子 对 爸爸 说："一定 是 妈妈 干 的。"

<small>Bàba wèn   Nǐ zěnme zhīdao</small>
爸爸 问："你 怎么 知道？"

<small>Érzi   shuō   Tā yī jù huà dōu méi shuō</small>
儿子 说："她 一 句 话 都 没 说。"

Translation

❷ Without Saying a Word

The mother and the daughter were doing the dishes after dinner while the father and the son were watching TV.

Suddenly, something fell clattering to the ground. But no more sound could be heard after that.

The son said to the father, 'It was Mom who did it.'

The father asked, 'How can you be so sure?'

The son answered, 'Because she didn't say a word.'

❸ Zěnme bàn
怎么办

Dìdi cóng xuéxiào huílai, bǎ chéngjìbiǎo gěi māma
弟弟 从 学校 回来，把 成绩表 给 妈妈
kàn。Māma kàn hòu hěn shēngqì。
看。妈妈 看 后 很 生气。

Tā duì dìdi shuō：Qùnián nǐ shì bānli de dì-yī,
她 对 弟弟 说："去年 你 是 班里 的 第一，
wǒ wèi nǐ gǎndào jiāo'ào。Jīnnián nǐ shì zěnme le
我 为 你 感到 骄傲。今年 你 是 怎么 了？"

Dìdi shuō：Měigè tóngxué de māma dōu xiǎng wèi
弟弟 说："每个 同学 的 妈妈 都 想 为
zìjǐ de háizi gǎndào jiāo'ào。Rúguǒ měi yī cì bānli
自己 的 孩子 感到 骄傲。如果 每 一 次 班里
de dì-yī dōu shì wǒ, tāmen de māma zěnme bàn
的 第一 都 是 我，他们 的 妈妈 怎么 办？"

Translation

❸ How to Handle It?

A boy came home from school and showed his report card to his mother. She got angry after going through it.

She said to her son, 'You took first place in class last year and I felt proud of you. What happened to you this year?'

Her son answered, 'Every mother wants to be proud of her kids. If I always take first place in class, how can the other mothers handle it?'

❹ Guò mǎlù
过 马路

Yǒu yī tiān, mèimei
有 一 天， 妹妹

gēn bàba shuō Bàba
跟 爸爸 说："爸爸，

māma shì bu shì hěn
妈妈 是 不 是 很

hàipà guò mǎlù a
害怕 过 马路 啊？"

Bàba wèn mèimei
爸爸 问 妹妹：

Nǐ wèishénme zhèyàng shuō
"你 为什么 这样 说？"

The road in the city

Mèimei shuō Měicì guò mǎlù māma zǒngshì jǐnzhāng de
妹妹 说："每次 过 马路， 妈妈 总是 紧张 地

lā zhe wǒ de shǒu bù fàng hái shuō bù yào líkāi wǒ
拉 着 我 的 手 不 放， 还 说 '不 要 离开 我。'"

Translation

❹ Crossing the Road

One day, a girl said to her father, 'Dad, is Mom afraid of crossing the road?'

Her father asked her, 'What makes you think so?'

She answered, 'Every time we cross the road, Mom always holds my hand nervously and even says something like "don't let go of me".'

❺ Qián
钱

Wáng tàitai hé Zhāng tàitai de háizi dōu shàng dàxué
王 太太 和 张 太太 的 孩子 都 上 大学

le
了。

Wáng tàitai shuō Wǒ hěn hàipà wǒ de érzi
王 太太 说："我 很 害怕，我 的 儿子

měicì dǎdiànhuà huíjiā dōu gēn wǒmen yào qián wǒ zhēnde
每次 打电话 回家 都 跟 我们 要 钱，我 真的

bù zhīdao tā yào nàme duō qián gànshénme
不 知道 他 要 那么 多 钱 干什么？"

Zhāng tàitai shuō Wǒ gèng hàipà wǒ de nǚ'ér
张 太太 说："我 更 害怕，我 的 女儿

cónglái bù gēn wǒmen
从来 不 跟 我们

yào qián wǒ zhēnde
要 钱，我 真的

bù zhīdao tā cóng
不 知道 她 从

nǎr nònglai qián
哪儿 弄来 钱！"

Renminbi

Translation

❺ Money

Mrs. Wang's and Mrs. Zhang's children are at university.

Mrs. Wang says, 'I'm worried. My son asks for money whenever he calls us. I haven't got a clue why he needs so much money.'

Mrs. Zhang replies, 'I'm more worried than you. My daughter never asks for money. I really have no idea where she gets her money!'

The Kind Mother (慈母 , *Cimu*)

'Kindness' (慈 , *ci*) means love in Chinese, referring to helping children grow up. Therefore, 'the kind mother (慈母)' is a term commonly used by the Chinese to describe a warm and loving mother who gives whatever she has to her kids. Mothers treat their children with kindness in virtually every aspect of life, for they have an infinite capacity for love.

However, the Chinese oppose the mother's indulging her children's every whim without properly disciplining them. A famous Chinese saying is 'a kind mother tends to spoil her son (慈母多败儿 , *cimuduobaier*)', which means if a loving mother is unduly protective towards her kids and does not discipline them in a proper manner, it's more than likely they may not achieve success. In this saying, 'kind mother (慈 母)' refers to mothers who over-indulge their children. When they notice that their kids have made mistakes, they agree with a smile trying to encourage and protect the children rather than discipline and correct them, even to the point of putting the blame on someone else. Since these children are not offered proper guidance, they will, without a doubt, have faults in their character and in the way they do things.

A mother and 8-year old daughter

GAMES FOR FUN

Chinese use some of the below words to praise mothers. Find the words.

认真 Earnest	暖和 Warm	可靠 Reliable
舒服 Comfortable	高级 Advanced	得意 Prideful
年轻 Young	好奇 Curious	精彩 Wonderful
快乐 Happy	漂亮 Beautiful	合适 Suitable

Xiānsheng   yǔ   tàitai

先生与太太

Husband and Wife

Pre-reading Questions

1. How should a couple get along with each other? Think about how your parents or friends are when they are together. Is there any room for improvement?

2. What kind of life would you like to have with your (future) husband/wife?

Tīng bù jìn
❶ 听不进

Zài bìngrén de fángjiān lǐmiàn
在 病人 的 房间 里面。

Hùshi shuō   Tàitai   qǐng nǐ shuōhuà qīng yīdiǎn hǎo
护士 说："太太，请 你 说话 轻 一点 好

ma   Nǐ de xiānsheng xūyào   xiūxi
吗？你 的 先生 需要 休息。"

Tā shuō   À   méi guānxi   Zhème duō nián le   wǒ
她 说："啊，没 关系。这么 多 年 了，我

de huà tā shì yī jù dōu tīng bù jìnqu de
的 话 他 是 一 句 都 听 不 进去 的。"

Translation

❶ To Fall on Deaf Ears

In a patient's hospital room.

The nurse says, 'Madam, could you please lower your voice? Your husband needs some rest.'

The woman answers, 'Oh, don't worry about it. For so many years, whatever I say to him always falls on deaf ears.'

❷ 没 时间

"你 跟 谁 在 门口 站 着，谈 了 三 个 小时 呢？"

"住 在 对面 的 张 太太。"

"怎么 不 请 她 进来 坐坐？"

"她 说 没有 时间。"

Translation

❷ Didn't Have Time

'Who were you talking with at the door for a good three hours?'

'Mrs. Zhang who lives across the street.'

'Why didn't you invite her in?'

'She said she didn't have time.'

❸ Xié 鞋

Wǎnfàn hòu
晚 饭 后，
yī gè nǚ tóngshì hē
一 个 女 同事 喝
duō le Chén xiānsheng
多 了，陈 先生
kāichē sòng tā huíjiā
开车 送 她 回家。

A cloth shoes in Chinese style

Huídào jiāli tā méiyǒu bǎ zhèjiàn shìqing gàosu
回到 家里，他 没有 把 这件 事情 告诉
tàitai
太太。

Dì-èr tiān zǎoshang Chén xiānsheng kāichē sòng tàitai
第二 天 早上，陈 先生 开车 送 太太
shàngbān Chēshang tā tūrán kàndào tàitai de jiǎo biān
上班。车上，他 突然 看到 太太 的 脚边，
yǒu yī zhī nǚrén de xié
有 一只 女人 的 鞋。

Zài tàitai shuìzháo de shíhou Chén xiānsheng gǎnjǐn
在 太太 睡着 的 时候，陈 先生 赶紧
náqi nà zhī xié diūdào chē wài
拿起 那只 鞋，丢到 车外。

Dào le gōngsī Chén tàitai tūrán dà jiào Wǒ de
到 了 公司，陈 太太 突然 大叫："我 的
xié ne
鞋 呢？"

Translation

❸ Shoe

After dinner, Mr. Chen drove a female colleague home. She had been drinking and was drunk.

He didn't tell his wife about it after returning home.

As he drove his wife to work the next morning, Mr. Chen noticed there was a woman's shoe next to her feet.

While his wife was dozing, Mr. Chen picked up the shoe hurriedly and threw it out of the car.

When they reached the company, Mrs. Chen woke up and shouted, 'Where's my shoe?'

❹ 关心
Guānxīn

Wǒ chūmén de shíhou zhǐ chuān le yī jiàn yīfu
我 出门 的 时候 只 穿 了 一 件 衣服。

Tā guānxīn wǒ shuō Wàimian hěn lěng xiǎoxīn
他 关心 我，说："外面 很 冷，小心

shēngbìng
生病。"

Wǒ shuō Méishì de wǒ bù lěng
我 说："没事 的，我 不 冷。"

Tā ná lai yī jiàn yīfu ràng wǒ chuānshàng shuō
他 拿 来 一 件 衣服 让 我 穿上，说：

Nǐ bié shēngbìng a Shàngcì nǐ shēngbìng le wǒ yī gè
"你 别 生病 啊！上次 你 生病 了，我 一 个

xīngqī méi fàn chī
星期 没 饭 吃！"

Translation

❹ Showing Consideration

I was only wearing a thin coat when I was about to go out.

My husband showed his consideration for me by saying, 'It's cold outside. Be careful not to get sick.'

I answered, 'Don't worry. I don't feel cold.'

He got a heavier coat, made me put it on, and then said, 'Don't let yourself get sick, okay? No one cooked for me for one week the last time you got sick.'

❺
Zhàopiàn
照片

Wáng tàitai zài fángjiān li, zhǎodào le yī zhāng Wáng
王 太太 在 房间 里, 找到 了 一 张 王

xiānsheng hé yī gè nǚrén de zhàopiàn
先生 和 一 个 女人 的 照片。

Wáng tàitai wèn Wáng xiānsheng Zhè shì zěnme huí
王 太太 问 王 先生:"这 是 怎么 回

shì
事?"

Wáng xiānsheng shuō Zhè shì liùniánqián de zhàopiàn Tā
王 先生 说:"这 是 六 年 前 的 照片。她

shì wǒ yǐqián de nǚpéngyou wǒ jǐ nián méi jiàn guo tā le
是 我 以前 的 女朋友,我 几 年 没 见 过 她 了。"

Wáng tàitai zhǐ zhe zhàopiàn dàshēng de shuō Zhèjiàn
王 太太 指 着 照片,大声 地 说:"这件

yīfu shì wǒ qùnián mǎi gěi nǐ de liùniánqián nǐ jiù
衣服 是 我 去年 买 给 你 的,六 年 前 你 就

chuānshàng le
穿上 了?"

Translation

❺ Photograph

Mrs. Wang found a photo of Mr. Wang with a woman.

Mrs. Wang asked Mr. Wang, 'What on earth is this?'

Mr. Wang answered, 'That photo was taken six years ago. She's my ex-girlfriend, and I haven't seen her for years.'

Mrs. Wang pointed at the photo and shouted, 'I bought you the clothe last year. You could wear them six years ago?'

❻ Shāngliang

商量

Zhāng xiānsheng xiàbān huíjiā   kàndào Zhāng tàitai de

张 先生 下班 回家，看到 张 太太 的

tóufa biàn duǎn le

头发 变 短 了。

Zhāng xiānsheng hěn bù gāoxìng de shuō   Nǐ bǎ zhème

张 先生 很 不 高兴 的 说："你 把 这么

A barber shop

cháng de tóufa nòng duǎn le zěnme bù xiān gēn wǒ shāngliang
长 的 头发 弄 短 了 , 怎么 不 先 跟 我 商量

yīxià
一下 ? "

Zhāng tàitai huí le yī jù Nǐ de tóufa dōu
张 太太 回 了 一 句 : " 你 的 头发 都

quánbù diào le shénme shíhou gěi wǒ shāngliang guo
全部 掉 了 , 什么 时候 给 我 商量 过 ! "

Translation

⑥ Discussion

Mr. Zhang came home from work, and he noticed that Mrs. Zhang had had her hair cut short.

Mr. Zhang complained, 'Why did you have your long hair cut short before talking to me about it?'

Mrs. Zhang shot back by saying, 'You lost all of your hair. When did you ever talk to me about that?'

Treating Each Other with Respect
(相敬如宾 , *Xiangjingrubin*)

For the Chinese, 'treating each other with respect (相敬如宾)' is the ideal relationship between husband and wife, which means husband and wife should treat each other as an honored guest.

This phrase comes from a story of ancient China. A man was weeding a field when his wife brought his lunch box to him in the field. She held up the box in both hands and respectfully gave it to him. In the same manner, the man solemnly received the box and ate his lunch deliberately. While he was eating lunch, his wife stood patiently by his side. When he finished, she cleared up, bid farewell to him politely, and then left. This couple treated each other with exactly the same etiquette that people used to greet and receive guests in ancient times. Their behavior was noticed by a high official who was

An old Chinese couple

passing by. He regarded the husband as a man of considerable culture, thus recommending him for an important post.

After you hear the story, you may feel confused, thinking: Is it necessary for two people living together to treat each other in such a polite way as attendants treat customers? In fact, this old Chinese saying does not emphasize external etiquette, but rather means that a couple should have mutual respect for each other. However, since it's easier said than done, this kind of respect should be inculcated and practiced in every detail of life.

Nán   yǔ   nǚ
男与女
Man and Woman

Pre-reading Questions

1. Write down 5 points that you think are essential to a relationship.

2. Apart from the 5 points written, think of 2 things about yourself which need to be changed, in order to have better relationships with others.

Tàiyáng   hé   yuèliang
❶ 太阳 和 月亮

　　Nǚhái   shuō　　　Nǐ   shì   wǒ   xīnzhōng   de   tàiyáng   gěi   wǒ
　女孩 说："你 是 我 心中 的 太阳，给 我

wēnnuǎn
温暖。"

　　Nánhái   shuō　　　Nǐ
　男孩 说："你

shì   tiānshàng   de   yuèliang
是 天上 的 月亮，

ràng   wǒ   de   shìjiè   yīpiàn
让 我 的 世界 一片

guāngmíng
光明 。"

A pair of mugs with "情侣" (lover)

25

Nǚhái tīng le zhè jù huà   tūrán   bù shuōhuà

女孩 听 了 这 句 话， 突然 不 说话，

bùyīhuìr   jiù kū qilai le

不一会儿 就 哭 起来 了。 ”

Nánhái hěn hàipà   wèn   Nǐ zěnme le

男孩 很 害怕， 问：“ 你 怎么 了？ ”

Nǚhái   kū zhe shuō   Tàiyáng hé yuèliang shì yǒngyuǎn

女孩 哭 着 说：“ 太阳 和 月亮 是 永远

bù kěnéng   zàiyīqǐ   de   nǐ shuō wǒmen de jiānglái hái yǒu

不 可能 在一起 的， 你 说 我们 的 将来 还 有

xīwàng ma

希望 吗？ ”

Translation

1 **The Sun and the Moon**

The girl says, 'You're the sun in my heart that keeps me warm.'

The boy says, 'You're the moon in the sky that brightens my world.'

After hearing this, the girl stops talking suddenly and then starts weeping.

Feeling concerned, the boy asks, 'What's the matter with you?'

The crying girl answers, 'The sun and the moon can never be together. Do you think we can still have a good future?'

❷ 不相信
Bù xiāngxìn

两个女孩正在讨论爱情是怎样来的。
Liǎng gè nǚhái zhèngzài tǎolùn àiqíng shì zěnyàng lái de

一个女孩说："不知道你怎么看，
Yī gè nǚhái shuō Bù zhīdao nǐ zěnme kàn

我不相信这个世界上，有第一次见面就
wǒ bù xiāngxìn zhège shìjièshang yǒu dì-yī cì jiànmiàn jiù

爱上他的事情。"
àishàng tā de shìqing

另外一个女孩问："为什么呢？"
Lìngwài yī gè nǚhái wèn Wèishénme ne

这个女孩说："你能第一次看到他，
Zhège nǚhái shuō Nǐ néng dì-yī cì kàndào tā

就知道他有车，有房子，有一份工资高
jiù zhīdao tā yǒu chē yǒu fángzi yǒu yī fèn gōngzī gāo

的工作吗？"
de gōngzuò ma

Translation

❷ Disbelief

Two girls are talking to each other about love.

One girl says, 'I don't know what you think of it, but I don't believe there is such a thing as love at first sight.'

The other girl asks, 'Why?'

The girl answers, 'Can you find out whether a man has a car, a house, and a well-paid job the first time you meet him?'

③ Shuō shénme
说 什么

Yī gè nánhái dì-yī
一 个 男孩 第一
cì gēn xǐhuan de nǚhái dào
次 跟 喜欢 的 女孩 到
wàimian chīfàn
外面 吃饭。

Paper-cut with the theme of Love

Chīfàn de shíhou
吃饭 的 时候,
nánhái zěnme dōu xiǎng bu chū yào gēn nǚhái shuō shénme
男孩 怎么 都 想 不 出 要 跟 女孩 说 什么。

Zhōngyú tā gēn nǚhái shuō chu le dì-yī jù huà
终于, 他 跟 女孩 说 出 了 第一 句 话:
Nǐ de bàba shēnghuó de zěnmeyàng
"你 的 爸爸 生活 得 怎么样?"

Nǚhái shuō Xièxie Tā hěn hǎo
女孩 说:"谢谢! 他 很 好"。

Nánhái shuō Māma ne
男孩 说:"妈妈 呢?"

Nǚhái shuō Yě hěn hǎo
女孩 说:"也 很 好。"

Nánhái shuō Gēge hé mèimei ne
男孩 说:"哥哥 和 妹妹 呢?"

Nǚhái shuō Xièxie Tāmen dōu shēnghuó de bùcuò
女孩 说:"谢谢! 他们 都 生活 得 不错。"

Nánhái tíng xialai méiyǒu huà yào shuō le
男孩 停 下来, 没有 话 要 说 了。

Zhèshíhou tā gàosu tā Wǒ háiyǒu yéye hé
这时候, 她 告诉 他:"我 还有 爷爷 和
nǎinai nín zěnme bù wèn le
奶奶, 您 怎么 不 问 了?"

Translation

❸ **What to Say**

A boy asked the girl he liked out on a date for the first time.

While they were having dinner, the boy couldn't think of anything to say to the girl, no matter how hard he tried.

Finally, he managed to squeeze out a sentence, saying, 'How is your father?'

The girl answered, 'Thank you! He's fine.'

The boy asked, 'And your mother?'

The girl answered, 'She's fine, too.'

The boy continued, 'How are your brothers and sisters?'

The girl replied, 'Thank you! They're all doing well.'

The boy stopped because he didn't know what to say next.

The girl then asked him, 'I still have a grandfather and a grandmother. How come you didn't ask me about them?'

❹ 怎样 走
Zěnyàng zǒu

一 个 男人 和 女朋友 到 公园 去。
Yī gè nánrén hé nǚpéngyou dào gōngyuán qù

来到 路口 的 时候，男人 说 要 往 东
Láidào lùkǒu de shíhou nánrén shuō yào wǎng dōng

走，女朋友 说 要 往 西 走。
zǒu nǚpéngyou shuō yào wǎng xī zǒu

两 个 人 都 认为 自己 是 对 的。
Liǎng gè rén dōu rènwéi zìjǐ shì duì de

这时候，一 个 朋友 刚刚 经过。男人 问
Zhèshíhou yī gè péngyou gānggāng jīngguò Nánrén wèn

他 该 怎样 走。
tā gāi zěnyàng zǒu

Zhège péngyou shuō Rúguǒ nǐ yào dào gōngyuán nǐ
这 个 朋 友 说 ：" 如 果 你 要 到 公 园 ， 你

yīnggāi wǎng dōng zǒu rúguǒ nǐ yào nǚpéngyou nǐ yīnggāi
应 该 往 东 走 ；如 果 你 要 女 朋 友 ， 你 应 该

wǎng xī zǒu
往 西 走 。"

Translation

4 **Which Way to Go**

A man and his girl friend were heading for a park.

When they came to an intersection, the man said they should go east, but his girl friend said they should go west.

Both of them thought they were right.

A friend of theirs passed by just at that moment, so the man asked him for directions.

His friend said, 'If you want to go to the park, you should go east. If you want to keep your girl friend, you should go west.'

The Post-80s (80 后 , *Bashihou*)

The younger generation in their twenties are called 'the post-80s (80 后)' in China. 'The post-80s' refers to the young people who were born in the 1980s. There are other similar terms like 'the post-70s (70 后)' and 'the post-90s (90 后)' which refer to the people born in the 1970s and 90s.

Because China introduced the one-child policy in 1979 and started the economic reforms in the eighties, the majority of young people belonging to the post-80s group are only children. The social environment they are experiencing is totally different from what their parents went through. This whole generation is vividly characterized by their individuality, a brand of the times put on them through the economic reforms.

How do the post-80s young adults form romantic relationships? A survey shows that campus love is quite popular. What motivates them to fall in love is to look for romance and life partners. Also, Internet romance is becoming a new way of choosing a mate. Unlike their parents, these young people are inclined to decide for themselves while seeking romance. They don't want others to interfere with their marriages. When it comes to the standard of choosing a mate, these post-80s young people are very pragmatic - personality and personal capacity are the qualities they value most. Facing huge competition and living under the pressures of modern life, more and more post-80s women are giving first priority to a man's capacity for creating wealth as well as his external accomplishments.

The Post-80s

GAMES FOR FUN

A "Love Knot" is a meaningful decorative knot with a long history in China. Meaning "love forever and devote yourselves to each other", a love knot is always used to symbolize the love between a man and a woman as the two knots are woven together.

This is how to weave a love knot. Try to make one and give it to your lover.

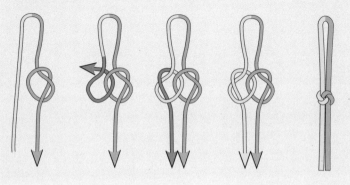

Jiào yǔ xué

教与学

Teaching and Learning

Pre-reading Questions

1. Does obtaining high scores in school really matter a great deal? Nowadays, people prefer to train well-rounded children instead of focusing only on the knowledge from textbooks, why?

2. What do you think is the most valuable aspect of schooling?

Tīng bù dǒng
❶ 听 不 懂

Chinese Sharpei

Lǎoshī shuō Míngtiān
老师 说 ： “ 明天

kāishǐ dàjiā shàngkè de
开始 ， 大家 上课 的

shíhou yào shǐyòng Yīngyǔ bù néng yòng Zhōngwén shuōhuà
时候 要 使用 英语 ， 不 能 用 中文 说话 。 ”

Tóngxué men dōu shuō Lǎoshī wǒmen de Yīngyǔ
同学 们 都 说 ： “ 老师 ， 我们 的 英语

tīnglì chà tīng bù dǒng a
听力 差 ， 听 不 懂 啊 。 ”

Lǎoshī shuō Bùyòng hàipà Nǐmen měitiān tīng wǒ
老师 说 ： “ 不用 害怕 。 你们 每天 听 我

shuō Yīngyǔ shíjiān jiǔ le jiù huì tīng dǒng
说 英语，时间 久 了 就 会 听 懂。"

Yī gè tóngxué shuō Lǎoshī wǒ měitiān dōu tīng wǒ
一 个 同学 说："老师，我 每天 都 听 我

jiā de xiǎo gǒu jiào Dào le jīntiān wǒ hái bù zhīdào tā
家 的 小 狗 叫。到 了 今天，我 还 不 知道 它

zài shuō shénme
在 说 什么。"

Translation

❶ Can't Understand

The teacher says, 'Starting from tomorrow, everyone must speak English in class. Chinese is not allowed.'

All the students respond by saying, 'Teacher, we are poor in listening. We don't understand English!'

The teacher answers, 'Don't be afraid. As long as you listen to me speaking English every day, you'll eventually understand it.'

One of the students says, 'Teacher, I listen to my puppy bark every day. But I still can't understand what it says.'

Wǒ zài tāmen zhōngjiān
❷ 我 在 他们 中间

Fàngxué hòu lǎoshī bǎ Xiǎo Wáng hé jǐ gè tóngxué liú
放学 后，老师 把 小 王 和 几 个 同学 留

xialai
下来。

Lǎoshī Zhècì kǎoshì wèishénme nǐmen kǎo de
老师："这次 考试，为什么 你们 考 得

^{zhème} ^{chà}
这 么 差 ？ ”

^{Tóngxué} ^{yī}　　　^{Wǒ} ^{kàn} ^{bù} ^{dào} ^{yuǎnchù} ^{de} ^{dōngxi}
同 学 一 ： “ 我 看 不 到 远 处 的 东西 ！ ”

^{Tóngxué} ^{èr}　　　^{Wǒ} ^{dài} ^{cuò} ^{le} ^{shū}
同 学 二 ： “ 我 带 错 了 书 。 ”

^{Tóngxué} ^{sān}　　　^{Qiánmiàn} ^{de} ^{tóngxué} ^{zhǎng} ^{de} ^{tài} ^{gāo} ^{le}
同 学 三 ： “ 前 面 的 同 学 长 得 太 高 了 。 ”

^{Tóngxué} ^{sì}　　　^{Pángbiān} ^{de} ^{tóngxué} ^{yòng} ^{qiānbǐ}　　^{wǒ} ^{kàn}
同 学 四 ： “ 旁 边 的 同 学 用 铅 笔 ， 我 看

^{bù} ^{qīngchu}
不 清 楚 。 ”

^{Lǎoshī} ^{tīng} ^{le} ^{hěn} ^{shēngqì}　　^{jiù} ^{wèn} ^{Xiǎo} ^{Wáng}　　　^{Nǐ} ^{ne}
老 师 听 了 很 生气， 就 问 小 王 ： “ 你 呢 ？ ”

^{Xiǎo} ^{Wáng}　　　^{Wǒ} ^{zuò} ^{zài} ^{tāmen} ^{sì} ^{gè} ^{zhōngjiān}
小 王 ： “ 我 坐 在 他 们 四 个 中 间 ……”

Translation

❷ **I was Surrounded by Them**

The teacher asked Xiao Wang and several other students to stay after school.

The teacher asked, 'How come all of you did so poorly on this test?'

Student A answered, 'I can't see stuff far away.'

Student B answered, 'I brought the wrong books.'

Student C answered, 'The student sitting in front of me is too tall.'

Student D answered, 'The student next to me wrote in pencil. I couldn't see the answers clearly.'

After hearing this, the teacher got very angry. Then, he asked Xiao Wang, 'How about you?'

Xiao Wang answered, 'I was surrounded by the four of them...'

❸ 字典 (Zìdiǎn)

课堂上，老师 说："在 我 的 人生 字典
里面，没有'失败'两 个 字！"

老师 刚 说 完，他 的 面前 马上 飞来 了
三十 多 本 字典。

同学们 一起
说："老师，我 的
借 你！"

【失败】shībài ❶在斗争
打败（跟'胜利'相对）：
定是要～的。❷工作没
的（跟'成功'相对）：～
【失策】shīcè ❶策略上
错误的策略。

"失败" — lose

Translation

❸ Dictionary

The teacher said to the class, 'In my dictionary, there is no such word as "failure"!'

Over thirty dictionaries were brought in front of the teacher immediately after he finished saying this.

The students said, 'Teacher, you can borrow mine!'

Kǎoshì
❹ 考试

Jǐ   gè   dàxué   nán
几 个 大学 男

tóngxué zǒu zài   yīqǐ
同学 走 在 一起。

Chinese students from the university

Tóngxué   yī
同学 一：

Nǐmen   zhīdao shénme shíhou kǎoshì ma
"你们 知道 什么 时候 考试 吗？"

Tóngxué èr   Dàgài shì xià gè xīngqī ba
同学 二："大概 是 下 个 星期 吧！"

Tóngxué sān   Hǎoxiàng hái yǒu jǐ tiān
同学 三："好像 还 有 几 天。"

Tóngxué sì   Jiù míngtiān kǎoshì
同学 四："就 明天 考试。"

Zhèshíhòu   yī   gè   nǚ   tóngxué zǒu guolai   Wèn
这时候， 一 个 女 同学 走 过来。 问：

Nǐmen   zuótiān wèishénme bù qù kǎoshì
"你们 昨天 为什么 不 去 考试？"

Translation

❹ Test

Several male college classmates are walking together.

Student A asks, 'Do you know when the test will be held?'

Student B answers, 'Probably the next week.'

Student C answers, 'There are a few more days to go, I guess.'

Student D answers, 'I'm sure it's tomorrow.'

Just then , one of their female classmates comes over and asks, 'How come none of you showed up for the test yesterday?'

❺ Shàngkè
上课

Yī gè dàxué lǎoshī zǒujìn jiàoshì Jiàoshì lǐmiàn
一个 大学 老师 走进 教室。教室 里面，

zhǐyǒu jǐ gè xuésheng zuò zhe
只有 几 个 学生 坐 着。

Lǎoshī hǎoxiàng méi kànjian yīyàng kāishǐ shàngkè
老师 好像 没 看见 一样，开始 上课。

Xiàkè de shíhou lǎoshī wèn Nǐmen jǐ gè de
下课 的 时候，老师 问："你们 几 个 的

xuéxí tàidu hěn bùcuò Nǐmen bān de qítā tóngxué jīntiān
学习 态度 很 不错。你们 班 的 其它 同学 今天

zěnme méi lái
怎么 没 来？"

Yī gè xuésheng shuō Lǎoshī wǒ yě bù zhīdao
一个 学生 说："老师，我 也 不 知道。

Wǒmen bùshì nǐ de xuésheng wǒmen zhǐshì zài zhèlǐ zuò
我们 不是 你 的 学生，我们 只是 在 这里 做

gōngkè
功课。"

Translation

❺ Attending Class

A university lecturer walked into a classroom. There were only a few students sitting there.

The lecturer started teaching as if he hadn't seen them.

When the class was over, the lecturer asked, 'You guys have a good learning attitude. How come the rest of the students in your class didn't show up?'

One of the students said, 'Teacher, I have no clue, either. We're not your students. We're just sitting here doing our homework.'

High Test Scores but Low Ability (高分低能 , *Gaofendineng*)

'High test scores but low ability (高分低能) ' is a term generally used to describe a phenomenon in which students are good at getting high scores in school education and on tests, but they have difficulty in dealing with situations in actual work and real lives, such as living independently, socializing, and innovating.

It is an indisputable fact that the test-oriented educational environment China developed has produced a large number of students who are good at 'getting high test scores but have low ability (高分低能)'. In 2005, 11 'top graduates (状元 , *zhuangyuan*)' who got the highest scores in Gao Kao, or the College Entrance Exam, held in the mainland were rejected from admission to the University of Hong Kong after the oral interview, simply because the university was unwilling to enroll 'nerds (书呆子 , *shudaizi*)' who are obsessed with learning but socially awkward.

The Chinese government is already aware of the issue in which the test-oriented educational system has produced many students who are good at 'getting high test scores but have low ability (高分低能)', which is why it keeps updating its concept of cultivating talent. The government has introduced measures to reform the educational system, asking teachers to combine learning with thinking during teaching sessions and to employ a variety of teaching methods in a flexible way in order to enhance students' self-learning ability and encourage them to apply knowledge to action. Moreover, attention has been directed to help students achieve their potential according to their personality differences. Since the start of the new century, China has been accelerating its pace in promoting education for all-round development. This newly designed basic education curriculum has been introduced to all the elementary schools and junior high schools across the nation.

Judging from the present situation, however, we can tell that the academic pressure brought to bear on students by Gao Kao is still the biggest barrier to bringing education for all-round development into practice. This shows that China's personnel appraisal system represented by Gao Kao still has flaws. The key to improvement is to firstly change the tendency of society to only hire highly educated employees and instead put more emphasis on the appraisal of candidates' practical abilities during the talent selection process.

Lǎobǎn yǔ zhígōng

老板与职工
Boss and Employee

Pre-reading Questions

1. Do you know that the minimum legal working age varies among countries?

2. What kind of career are you looking for?

3. Make an interview question list. Then ask and answer each question yourself before you go for an interview.

Sān gè rén de gōngzuò
❶ 三 个 人 的 工 作

Yī gè lǎo zhígōng
一 个 老 职 工

hěn shēngqì de duì lǎobǎn
很 生 气 地 对 老 板

shuō Lǎobǎn wǒ zài
说："老 板，我 在

Factory in China

zhèlǐ shí duō nián le Wǒ yī gè rén zuò le sān gè rén
这 里 十 多 年 了。我 一 个 人 做 了 三 个 人

de gōngzuò wǒ zhǐ nádào yī gè rén de gōngzī
的 工 作，我 只 拿 到 一 个 人 的 工 资。"

Lǎobǎn shuō　　　Nǐ xiǎng zěnmeyàng ne
老板 说：“你 想 怎么样 呢？”

Lǎo zhígōng shuō　　　Wǒ qǐngqiú zēngjiā gōngzī
老 职工 说：“我 请求 增加 工资。”

Lǎobǎn shuō　　　Hǎo de dàn yǒu yī gè tiáojiàn　Nǐ
老板 说：“好 的，但 有 一 个 条件。你

yào xiān shuō chu nà liǎng gè rén shì shuí
要 先 说 出 那 两 个 人 是 谁。”

Translation

❶ Three Employees' Workload

A veteran employee said to his boss angrily, 'Boss, I've been working here for more than ten years. I do the work of three employees, but I just get paid for only one employee's work.'

The boss asked, 'What do you want me to do?'

The employee answered, 'I want a salary increase.'

The boss said, 'Okay. I'll do it, but there's one condition. You must tell me who the other two employees are.'

Gōngzuò
❷ 工作

Chén xiǎojiě shēngbìng jìn le yīyuàn　Jǐ gè nǚ
陈 小姐 生病，进 了 医院。几 个 女

tóngshì yīqǐ qiánwǎng tànwàng
同事 一起 前往 探望。

Chén xiǎojiě shuō　　　Duìbuqǐ wǒ liú xialai de
陈 小姐 说：“对不起，我 留 下来 的

gōngzuò yīdìng bǎ nǐmen lèi huài le
工作 一定 把 你们 累 坏 了。”

Yī　gè　nǔ　tóngshì　xiào　zhe　shuō　　Hái　hǎo　ba　　nǐ
一 个 女 同事 笑 着 说："还 好 吧，你

de　gōngzuò　dàjiā　　yīqǐ　zuò　le　　Wǒ　fùzé　kàn　bàozhǐ
的 工作 大家 一起 做 了。我 负责 看 报纸，

Wáng　xiǎojiě　dǎdiànhuà　zhǎo　péngyou　Lǐ　xiǎojiě　shàngwǎng　mǎi
王 小姐 打电话 找 朋友，李 小姐 上网 买

dōngxi　Zhāng　xiǎojiě　dàochù　shōu　xiāoxi
东西，张 小姐 到处 收 消息。"

Translation

❷ Work

Ms. Chen was sick and hospitalized. Several of her female colleagues went to visit her.

Ms. Chen said, 'I'm sorry. The work I left behind must have worn you out.'

One of the colleagues laughed and said, 'I think that's okay. We shared your work. I read newspapers. Ms. Wang made phone calls to her friends. Ms. Lee did shopping online. And Ms. Zhang spent a lot of time poking and prying.'

Bùhǎoshuō
❸ 不好说

Lǎobǎn　　　Nǐ　duì　gōngsī　yǒu　shénme　yìjiàn　ne
老板："你 对 公司 有 什么 意见 呢？"

Zhígōng　　　Bùhǎoshuō
职工："不好说。"

Lǎobǎn　　　Bù　yào　xiǎng　tài　duō　　shuō　ba
老板："不要 想 太 多，说 吧。"

Zhígōng　　　Bù　shuō　hǎo
职工："不 说 好。"

Lǎobǎn　　　Nǐ bùyào hàipà　fàngxīn shuō ba
老板：“你 不 要 害怕，放心 说 吧。”

Zhígōng　　　Shuō bù hǎo
职工：“说 不 好。”

Translation

❸ Hard to Say

The boss asks, 'What's your opinion of the company?'

The employee answers, 'It's hard to say.'

The boss says, 'Don't think too much. Just tell me what's on your mind.'

The employee says, 'It's better not to say.'

The boss asks again, 'Don't be afraid. Relax and tell me.'

The employee answers, 'I have a problem saying exactly what I think.'

Cānjiā　kǎoshì
❹ 参加 考试

Wáng xiānsheng kāi le yī gè xiǎo gōngsī　Gōngsī dǎ chu
王 先生 开 了 一 个 小 公司。公司 打 出

guǎnggào hòu　　shōudào le hěnduō xìn
广告 后，收到 了 很多 信。

Wáng xiānsheng xuǎnzhòng le yī gè nǚshēng　dǎdiànhuà ràng
王 先生 选中 了 一 个 女生，打电话 让

tā lái cānjiā kǎoshì
她 来 参加 考试。

Tā yǐwéi duìfāng huì hěn gāoxìng　méi xiǎngdào duìfāng
他 以为 对方 会 很 高兴，没 想到 对方

lěnglěngde wèn　Gōngsī zài shénme dìfang ne
冷冷地 问：“公司 在 什么 地方 呢？”

Wáng xiānsheng shuō le dìzhǐ
王 先生 说 了 地址。

Nǚshēng shuō Zhème yuǎn
女生 说："这么 远,

zěnme qù a
怎么 去 啊?"

Wáng xiānsheng yǒudiǎnr bù
王 先生 有点儿 不

gāoxìng le háishi shuō xiaqu
高兴 了, 还是 说 下去:

Recruitments of Chinese factories

Zuò gōngjiāochē dǎchē dōu xíng
"坐 公交车、打车 都 行。"

Méixiǎngdào nǚshēng huí le yī jù Tài yuǎn le nǐ
没想到 女生 回 了 一 句:"太 远 了, 你

kāichē lái jiē wǒ hǎo ma
开车 来 接 我 好 吗?"

Translation

❹ Taking an Exam

Mr. Wang owned a small company. After a hiring advertisement was published, the company received many job applications.

Mr. Wang chose a female applicant and then called her telling her to to come for an interview.

He thought the girl would be very happy. Instead, she answered in a cold voice, 'Where is your company?'

Mr. Wang told her the address.

The girl said, 'It's far away. How can I get there?'

Mr. Wang felt annoyed, but he managed to say, 'You can either take the bus or hire a taxi.'

Surprisingly, the girl answered, 'It's too far away. Can you come and pick me up?'

❺ 正是 时候
Zhèngshì shíhou

李 先生 走到 老板
Lǐ xiānsheng zǒudào lǎobǎn

面前。
miànqián

他 很 不 开心 地 说：
Tā hěn bù kāixīn de shuō

"老板，我 已经 六十 多
Lǎobǎn wǒ yǐjing liùshí duō

了。我 感到 我 的 工作
le Wǒ gǎndào wǒ de gōngzuò

不 能 做 下去 了。"
bù néng zuò xiaqu le

老板 问："为什么 呢？"
Lǎobǎn wèn Wèishénme ne

李 先生 说："我 的 听力 越来越 差，我
Lǐ xiānsheng shuō Wǒ de tīnglì yuèláiyuè chà wǒ

听 不 清楚 顾客 对 我 说 什么 了。"
tīng bù qīngchu gùkè duì wǒ shuō shénme le

老板 说："没 关系，我 正要 调 你 到
Lǎobǎn shuō Méi guānxì wǒ zhèngyào diào nǐ dào

意见台 去。"
yìjiàntái qù

The service center of a shopping mall

Translation

❺ Just the Right Time

Mr. Lee went up to his boss.

He said unhappily, 'Boss, I'm over sixty years old. I feel I'm not capable of doing my job any more.'

The boss asked, 'Why?'

Mr. Lee answered, 'My hearing is getting worse and worse. I can't hear clearly what customers say to me.'

The boss replied, 'That's totally fine. I'm thinking of transferring you to the complaints department.'

Iron Rice Bowl (铁饭碗 , *Tiefanwan*)

The iron rice bowl, as implied by the term, literally means a rice bowl made of iron that is robust and unbreakable. In China, the meaning of this term is extended to refer to an ideal occupation or position with steady income, substantial benefits, and an excellent working environment. For a long time, people have had the impression that if you have an iron rice bowl, you will live a worry-free life; on the contrary, if you don't have an iron rice bowl, you will live a life full of hard work and worry, with very little pleasure and peace during your whole life. The 'iron rice bowl' concept is deeply rooted in Chinese philosophy, and it is a life goal that many Chinese people are pursuing.

The term 'iron rice bowl (铁饭碗)' was coined just as China introduced its economic reform. At that time, the majority of businesses were state run, where everyone's employment was guaranteed – it didn't matter how much work they had done or how lousy their job performance was. The wages increased on schedule and the benefits were paid based on the number of employees. Almost every business was overstaffed. The surplus staff slowed down the pace of the businesses' development, becoming a huge burden on the enterprises and adversely affecting people's enthusiasm for work.

Some people finally claimed that the state run businesses, or even China as a whole, could never find a way out if the idea of the 'iron rice bowl' was not broken. In fact, what needs to be broken are the inefficient and

An iron rice bowl is not easily broken. Thus it is a symbol of a stable career.

unfair 'iron rice bowls'. Meanwhile, an 'iron rice bowl' system for all and guaranteed by society needs to be rebuilt on a complete and fair basis. Under this system, everyone is required to face the question of how to secure their own job.

Nowadays, more and more people are realizing that only by doing all they can to catch up, improving themselves and enriching their lives will they be able to make a 'golden rice bowl' which guarantees their 'employability' for a long time to come. This is a real long-term life plan that will help establish a foothold for them to achieve their aims.

GAMES FOR FUN

How would you answer the question below in a recruitment interview?

You are driving on a stormy night.

You pass by a bus station.

There are three people waiting for the bus.

One of them is a pitiful dying old man.

The other is a doctor who once saved your life, and you want to repay his favor.

The last one is a woman/man who you dream to marry and you want to grab a chance to know her .

However, your car can only take one more extra passenger. What would you do?

Answer:
The best solution is to give the car key to the doctor so he can drive the old person to hospital and you stay with your dream lover to wait for the bus.

Yīshēng   yǔ   bìngrén

医生与病人

Doctor and Patient

Pre-reading Questions

1. Western medicine and traditional Chinese medicine use two different approaches to cure patients. Do you know the differences?

2. Traditional Chinese medicine is usually made from plants called herbs. Can you name a few plants that are herbs?

Yǎnbìng
❶ 眼病

Bìngrén shuō   Wǒ
病人 说 ： “ 我

de   dùzi   hěn téng
的 肚子 很 疼 。 ”

Yīshēng wèn   Nǐ
医生 问 ： “ 你

jīntiān chī le shénme ne
今天 吃 了 什么 呢 ？ ”

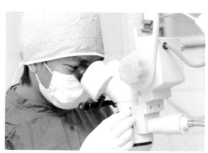

A doctor of ophthalmology

Bìngrén shuō   Wǒ chī le   yīxiē   bù   gānjìng de
病人 说 ： “ 我 吃 了 一些 不 干净 的

dōngxi
东西 。 ”

48

Yīshēng shénme huà dōu méi shuō   gěi bìngrén yīxiē zhì
医生 什么 话 都 没 说，给 病人 一些 治

yǎn de yào
眼 的 药。

Bìngrén hěn qíguài   wèn   Dàifu   zhèxiē yào yǒuyòng
病人 很 奇怪，问："大夫，这些 药 有用

ma
吗？"

Yīshēng shuō   Yǒuyòng   Nǐ de yǎn zhì hǎo le   nǐ
医生 说："有用。你 的 眼 治 好 了，你

jiù néng kàn qīngchu chī de shì shénme dōngxi
就 能 看 清楚 吃 的 是 什么 东西。"

Translation

❶ Eye Disease

The patient said, 'My stomach is aching.'

The doctor asked, 'What did you eat today?'

The patient replied, 'I ate some unclean stuff.'

The doctor didn't say anything. He just prescribed some eye medications for the patient.

Feeling uncertain , the patient asked, 'Doctor, do these medications work?'

The doctor answered, 'Of course, they do. When you get your eye disease cured, then you can see clearly what you eat.'

❷ 交费

Yī gè bìngrén duì péngyou shuō　　Wǒ zhè jǐtiān zǒngshì
一 个 病人 对 朋友 说："我 这 几天 总是

jìbuzhù shìqing Shàngwǔ de shì xiàwǔ jiù wàng le
记不住 事情。上午 的 事，下午 就 忘 了。"

Péngyou　　　Nǐ kàn le yīshēng méiyǒu
朋友："你 看 了 医生 没有？"

Bìngrén　　　Kàn le
病人："看 了。"

Péngyou　　　Yīshēng zěnme shuō
朋友："医生 怎么 说？"

Bìngrén　　Tā shuō wǒ bìxū xiān jiāofèi cáinéng kànbìng
病人："他 说 我 必须 先 交费，才能 看病。"

Péngyou　　　Wèishénme ne
朋友："为什么 呢？"

Bìngrén　　　Tā pà wǒ wàng le jiāofèi
病人："他 怕 我 忘 了 交费。"

Translation

❷ **Making Payment**

A patient says to his friend, 'I haven't been able to remember anything over the past few days. What happens to me in the morning, I forget it in the afternoon.'

His friend says, 'Did you see a doctor?'

The patient answers, 'Yes, I did.'

The friend asks, 'What did the doctor say?'

The patient answers, 'He said I must pay before receiving treatment.'

The friend asks, 'Why?'

The patient answers, 'He was afraid that I would forget to pay.'

❸ 不要害怕
Bù yào hàipà

一 个 病人 上午 进 了 医院，准备 下午
Yī gè bìngrén shàngwǔ jìn le yīyuàn zhǔnbèi xiàwǔ

动手术。
dòngshǒushù

不 到 中午，他 就 离开 了。
Bù dào zhōngwǔ tā jiù líkāi le

回到 家里，病人 对 太太 说："我 不
Huídào jiāli bìngrén duì tàitai shuō Wǒ bù

动手术 了。"
dòngshǒushù le

太太 问："为什么 呢？"
Tàitai wèn Wèishénme ne

病人 说："我 听到 护士 说'不 要 害怕，
Bìngrén shuō Wǒ tīngdào hùshi shuō bù yào hàipà

手术 很 简单。'"
shǒushù hěn jiǎndān

太太 说："这 句 话 不 对 吗？"
Tàitai shuō Zhè jù huà bù duì ma

病人 说："她 是 对 医生 说 的！"
Bìngrén shuō Tā shì duì yīshēng shuō de

Translation

❸ Don't be Afraid

A man was sent to a hospital in the morning, waiting for surgery in the afternoon.

However, he left before noon.

When he came home, the man said to his wife, 'I don't want to have the surgery.'

His wife asked, 'Why?'

The man answered, 'I heard the nurse say "Don't be afraid. The surgery is very easy".'

His wife said, 'Is there anything wrong with that?'

The man replied, 'It's what she said to the doctor!'

❹ Duōcháng shíjiān
多 长 时间

Yīshēng　　Nín de tóu duō cháng shíjiān téng yī cì
医生："您 的 头 多 长 时间 疼 一 次？"

Bìngrén　　Měi wǔ fēnzhōng jiù téng yī cì
病人："每 五 分钟 就 疼 一 次。"

Yīshēng　　Nàme měicì téng duō cháng shíjiān
医生："那么，每次 疼 多 长 时间"？

Bìngrén　　Zhìshǎo shíwǔ fēnzhōng
病人："至少 十五 分钟。"

Translation

❹ **How Long Does It Last?**

The doctor asks, 'How often does your headache throb?'

The patient answers, 'Every five minutes.'

The doctor asks, 'Then, how long does it last?'

The patient replies, 'At least fifteen minutes.'

❺ 谁在害怕
Shuí zài hàipà

一个 病人
Yī gè bìngrén

得 了 病，要
dé le bìng yào

动手术。
dòngshǒushù

The doctors who are having an operation

他 心里 很
Tā xīnli hěn

害怕。他 要求 做 手术 的 医生 和 护士 不 能
hàipà Tā yāoqiú zuò shǒushù de yīshēng hé hùshi bù néng

用 口罩。
yòng kǒuzhào

医生 不 同意，说："这 是 医院 的 规定。"
Yīshēng Bù tóngyì shuō Zhè shì yīyuàn de guīdìng

病人 说："别 找 理由 了。你们 害怕 出
Bìngrén shuō Bié zhǎo lǐyóu le Nǐmen hàipà chū

了 意外，怕 我 知道 你们 是 谁 吧!"
le yìwài pà wǒ zhīdao nǐmen shì shuí ba

Translation

❺ Who is Afraid?

A man was sick and he needed surgery.

He was very afraid, so he requested that the doctor and the nurses who were to conduct the surgery should not wear gauze masks.

The doctor disagreed, saying, 'This is the hospital's rule.'

The man replied, 'Don't make an excuse. You're afraid that I'll recognize you if an accident happens!'

❻ 睡觉

Shuìjiào

Yī gè bìngrén duì yīshēng shuō   Dàifu wǒ báitiān
一 个 病 人 对 医 生 说:"大 夫, 我 白 天

hěn xiǎng shuìjiào   yīdào wǎnshang jiù zěnme dōu shuì bù zháo
很 想 睡 觉, 一 到 晚 上 就 怎 么 都 睡 不 着。

Zhège bìng néng zhì hǎo ma
这 个 病 能 治 好 吗?"

Yīshēng shuō   Zhì nǐ de bìng hěn jiǎndān   yě hěn
医 生 说:"治 你 的 病 很 简 单, 也 很

róngyì
容 易。"

Bìngrén shuō   Yǒu shénme hǎo fāngfǎ ne
病 人 说:"有 什 么 好 方 法 呢?"

Yīshēng shuō   Cóng jīntiān kāishǐ   nǐ wǎnshang
医 生 说:"从 今 天 开 始, 你 晚 上

gōngzuò báitiān shuìjiào jiù kěyǐ le
工 作, 白 天 睡 觉 就 可 以 了。"

Translation

❻ Sleep

A patient says to a doctor, 'Doctor, I feel sleepy during the day, but I can't fall asleep at night. Is it possible to cure my disease?'

The doctor answers, 'It's quite simple and easy to cure your disease.'

The patient says, 'What's your treatment?'

The doctor replies, 'Starting from today, you work at night and sleep during the day.'

Skin Scraping (刮痧 , *Guasha*)

A movie titled 'Skin Scraping' was a smash hit several years ago. It tells the story of a grandfather who tries to cure his grandson's illness with the practice of skin scraping, only to arouse suspicions of child abuse. This reflects the conflicts and contradictions faced by overseas Chinese due to cultural differences between East and West. After it was released, the film not only caused people to reflect on the issue, but also evoked people's intense interest in 'Skin Scraping'.

'Skin Scraping' is not a secret practice. In fact, it is a traditional Chinese medical treatment. The earliest record of 'Skin Scraping' occurred in 1337 AD. The character 'sha' (痧) evolves from 'sand'(沙 , *sha*), referring to an illness. The 'Skin Scraping' technique is employed to remove the toxins of 'sha' (痧) (namely viruses) from the body to cure a disease. It can be used to scrape away many kinds of diseases, and 'sandy-looking' spots with different colors, such as red, purple red, and dark blue, will appear on patients' skin after they have received the treatment, hence the name of 'Skin Scraping'. The conflicts depicted in the film originate from this.

The practice of 'Skin Scraping' uses tools like an ox horn and a jade stone to scrape specific areas on the skin. This is done to expand capillaries, increase the secretion of sweat glands, and improve blood circulation, with the aim of dredging meridians and facilitating blood circulation, for example to cure bruises. Moreover, 'Skin

Gua Sha Treatment

Scraping' can be used to treat all sorts of illnesses caused by exposure to wind and cold with instant and amazing results. 'Skin Scraping' has now become a very popular treatment because it is easy to learn, easy to administer and very effective in curing diseases.

GAMES FOR FUN

Traditional Chinese medical science has a three thousand year history , and is still adopted by the Chinese today . The ingredients of Chinese medicine are mostly made from plants.

Some of the ingredients used in Chinese medicines are below. Can you recognize them?

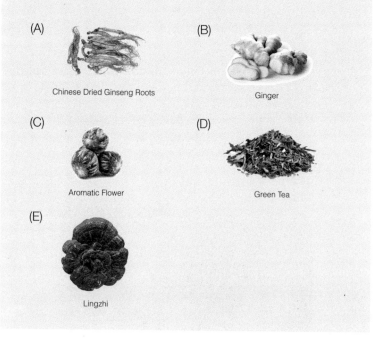

(A)

Chinese Dried Ginseng Roots

(B)

Ginger

(C)

Aromatic Flower

(D)

Green Tea

(E)

Lingzhi

Answer:
A and E are Chinese medicines.
B is a commonly used Chinese cooking ingredient.
C and D are teas that Chinese frequently drink.

Kèrén　　yǔ　　fúwùyuán
客人与服务员
Customer and Attendant

Pre-reading Questions

1. When you need to choose a restaurant to dine out which concerns you most, food quality, service or price?

2. Some chain restaurants have different menus in various countries, to suit different taste preferences. Can you name any restaurants having this feature of different menus?

Dàxiǎo　bùtóng
❶ 大小 不同

Wáng xiānsheng láidào yī jiān yǒumíng de fàndiàn chīfàn
王 先生 来到 一 间 有名 的 饭店 吃饭。

Tā diǎn de shíwù dào le Tā kànguo hòu hěn bù
他 点 的 食物 到 了。他 看过 后, 很 不

gāoxìng
高兴。

Wáng xiānsheng duì fúwùyuán shuō Wèishénme tóngyàng de
王 先生 对 服务员 说:"为什么 同样 的

shíwù wǒ jīntiān chī de bǐ zuótiān de shǎo yībàn ne
食物, 我 今天 吃 的 比 昨天 的 少 一半 呢?"

Fúwùyuán shuō Duìbuqǐ xiānsheng qǐngwèn nǐ
服务员 说:"对不起, 先生, 请问 你

zuótiān zuò zài nǎr ne
昨天 坐 在 哪儿 呢？"

　　Wáng xiānsheng shuō Wǒ zuótiān zuò zài chuāngzi
　　王 先生 说："我 昨天 坐 在 窗子

pángbiān
旁边。"

　　Fúwùyuán shuō Nà jiù duì le Xiānsheng wǒmen
　　服务员 说："那 就 对 了。先生，我们

huì gěi zuò zài chuāngzl pángbiān de kèrén sòngshàng duō yī bèi
会 给 坐 在 窗子 旁边 的 客人 送上 多 一 倍

de shíwù zhè shì hěn hǎo de guǎnggào a
的 食物。这 是 很 好 的 广告 啊。"

Translation

❶ Different Amount of Food

Mr. Wang dined out at a popular restaurant.

When his order was served, he took a look at it and felt disappointed.

Mr. Wang said to the waiter, 'I ordered the same meal yesterday. Why do you serve only half the amount today?'

The waiter asked, 'Sir, I'm sorry. May I ask where you sat yesterday?'

Mr. Wang answered, 'I sat next to the window yesterday.'

The waiter replied, 'That's right, sir. We give double the amount of food to customers sitting next to the window. It's a good way of advertising.'

　　Bāozi li yǒu rén
❷ 包子 里 有 人

　　Yī gè rén zài fàndiàn chī bāozi
　　一 个 人 在 饭店 吃 包子。

Tā chī zhe chī zhe
他 吃 着 吃 着，
hūrán hǎndào Ā zhè
忽然 喊道："啊，这
bāozi li yǒu rén
包子 里 有 人！"

Chinese bread

Gùkèmen tīngdào le
顾客们 听到 了，
dōu wéi guolai kàn
都 围 过来 看。

Fúwùyuán kànguo hòu hěn shēngqì shuō Xiānsheng
服务员 看过 后，很 生气，说："先生，
bāozi lǐmiàn nǎli yǒu rén ne
包子 里面 哪里 有 人 呢？"

Nàrén shuō Nǐ shuō bāozi lǐmiàn méi rén zěnme
那人 说："你 说 包子 里面 没 人，怎么
lǐmiàn yǒu rén de tóufa ne
里面 有 人 的 头发 呢？"

Translation

❷ **There is a person in the steamed bun**

A man is eating steamed buns at a restaurant

While he is enjoying them, the man cries out suddenly, 'My god! There's a person in the steamed bun.'

Hearing this, other customers immediately surround him to have a look.

However, the waiter is angry after checking the bun, saying, 'Sir, why on earth did you say there's a person in the steamed bun?'

The man answers, 'You claim there's no one in the steamed bun. But how come there's hair in it?'

❸ Bēizi
杯子

Fúwùyuán wèn: Liǎng wèi, qǐngwèn yào hē shénme
服务员 问："两 位，请问 要 喝 什么

ne?
呢？"

Yī gè kèrén shuō: Gěi wǒ yī bēi chá!
一 个 客人 说："给 我 一 杯 茶！"

Lìngwài yī gè kèrén shuō: Wǒ yě yīyàng, qǐng bǎ
另外 一 个 客人 说："我 也 一样，请 把

bēizi nòng gānjìng diǎn!
杯子 弄 干净 点！"

Fúwùyuán shuō: Hǎo de, qǐng děng yi děng.
服务员 说："好 的，请 等 一 等。"

Guò le yīhuìr. Fúwùyuán wèn: Duìbuqǐ,
过 了 一会儿。服务员 问："对不起，

qǐngwèn gāngcái nǎwèi yào gānjìng de bēizi?
请问 刚才 哪位 要 干净 的 杯子？"

Translation

❸ Cup

The waiter asks, 'Sirs, what would you like to drink?'

One customer says, 'Give me a cup of tea!'

The other customer says, 'Same for me. But please clean the cup!'

The waiter answers, 'Yes, please wait a minute.'

After a while, the waiter asks, 'Excuse me, which one of you asked for a clean cup?'

❹ 蛋糕
Dàngāo

Wáng xiānsheng qǐng Lǐ xiānsheng chīfàn
王 先生 请 李 先生 吃饭。

Chī wán fàn hòu fúwùyuán zǒu guolai shuō Nǐmen
吃 完 饭 后，服 务 员 走 过 来，说："你们

hái xūyào lái diǎn dàngāo ma
还 需要 来 点 蛋糕 吗？"

Lǐ xiānsheng shuō Wǒ yào yī kuài dàngāo
李 先生 说："我 要 一 块 蛋糕。"

Wáng xiānsheng shuō Xièxie wǒ zài yě chī bu xià
王 先生 说："谢谢，我 再 也 吃 不 下

le
了"

Fúwùyuán shuō Jīntiān de dàngāo shì sòng de
服务员 说："今天 的 蛋糕 是 送 的。"

Wáng xiānsheng shuō Gěi wǒ lái liǎng kuài dàngāo ba
王 先生 说："给 我 来 两 块 蛋糕 吧。"

Translation

❹ Cake

Mr. Wang treated Mr. Lee to dinner.

After they finished eating the meal, the waiter came over and asked, 'Would you like some cakes?'

Mr. Lee said, 'I'd like a cake.'

Mr. Wang said, 'No, thank you! I'm stuffed.'

The waiter said, 'Cakes are on the house today, sir.'

Mr. Wang said, 'Well then, just give me two cakes.'

❺ 到 外面 吃饭
Dào wàimian chīfàn

李 先生 到 一 家 饭店
Lǐ xiānsheng dào yī jiā fàndiàn

吃饭。 饭 吃 了 一半，李
chīfàn Fàn chī le yībàn Lǐ

先生 就 停 了 下来，吃 不
xiānsheng jiù tíng le xiàlái chī bu

下去。
xiàqù

李 先生 找 来 服务员，
Lǐ xiānsheng zhǎo lai fúwùyuán

A happy gathering

很 不 高兴 地 说："你们 这里 食物 的 味道 太
hěn bù gāoxìng de shuō Nǐmen zhèlǐ shíwù de wèidao tài

差 了，我 要 见 你们 的 老板。"
chà le wǒ yào jiàn nǐmen de lǎobǎn

服务员 说："对不起，现在 是 午饭
Fúwùyuán shuō Duìbuqǐ xiànzài shì wǔfàn

时间，我们 的 老板 到 外面 吃饭 去 了。"
shíjiān wǒmen de lǎobǎn dào wàimian chīfàn qù le

Translation

❺ Dinning out

Mr. Lee ate out at a restaurant. He stopped half way through because he couldn't bear to swallow the remaining meal any more.

Mr. Lee called for the waiter and complained, 'The food is lousy. I want to see your manager.'

The waiter replied, 'I'm sorry, sir. It's lunch break now. Our manager is eating at another restaurant.'

Smiling Service

Business competition in China is now very keen. To secure a position, businesses are providing service with a smile one after another in the hope that they may win more customers. This is especially true in the service industry.

'Smiles' can always shorten the distance between people, giving customers an impression of feeling at home. When an attendant smiles at a customer, what the attendant is trying to convey is: 'It's so nice to meet you and I'm pleased to serve you.' In view of this, providing smiles with service is already set out as a basic requirement for the employees in many Chinese businesses in order to improve service quality.

Everyone can smile, but it is much more difficult to give a winning, natural smile. How on earth can one train oneself to give sincere smiles? 'At the beginning, I was unable to smile at strangers. I either gave shy smiles or forced tight smiles,' said an attendant rated as 'The Star of Smiles' for her service.

Afterwards, she held chopsticks in her mouth for a long time to practice the loveliest 'eight teeth' smile. Sometimes her facial muscle would convulse with too much practice and her saliva would keep dripping down. To practice the standard standing gesture, she would either stand with her back pressed against the wall or stand back to back with her colleague with a slip of paper between them, practicing for hours on end. Because she could only spare limited time during working hours, she would look at herself in the mirror and practice repeatedly after she went home.

To get one thing done well, you must give the corresponding amount of hard work. Although it might be painful to go through the process, you will get what you deserve as long as you keep persevering in your efforts.

A smiling waitress

Mǎi   yǔ   mài
买与卖
Buying and Selling

Pre-reading Questions

1. Do you know how to be a smart customer? Suggest 3 points to note during a transaction.

2. Sometimes it is normal practice to bargain. Besides enjoying the atmosphere, you may buy the product at a lower price. Try it next time!

Mǎi yú
❶ 买鱼

Chén xiānsheng dào shìchǎng
陈 先生 到 市场

qù mǎi yú   Tā ná qǐ yī
去买鱼。他拿起一

tiáo yú   wén le   yīxià
条鱼，闻了一下。

Fishes in chinese supermarket

Mài yú de rén hěn bù gāoxìng   duì Chén xiānsheng shuō
卖鱼的人很不高兴，对陈先生说：

Xiānsheng nǐ bù mǎi yú méi guānxi   nǐ wén shénme ne
"先生，你不买鱼没关系，你闻什么呢？"

陈 先生 说：“我 不 是 闻，我 是 跟 鱼
说话。”

卖 鱼 的 人 说：“你 跟 鱼 说 什么 呢？”

陈 先生 说：“我 问 鱼，海 里面 最近 有
什么 大 新闻。”

卖 鱼 的 人 说：“鱼 怎么 说 呢？”

陈 先生 说：“它 说 不 知道，它 离开
海 已经 很 久 了。”

Translation

1 Buying Fish

Mr. Chen went to the market to buy fish. He picked up a fish and smelled it.

The fishmonger was annoyed and complained to Mr. Chen, Sir, you didn't buy the fish, and that's fine with me. But what were you trying to find out by smelling it?'

Mr. Chen replied, 'I did not smell the fish. I chatted with it.'

The fishmonger asked, 'What did you say to it?'

Mr. Chen answered, 'I asked the fish about the latest big news in the sea .'

The fishmonger asked, 'What did it say?'

Mr. Chen said, 'The fish said it had no idea. It's been away from the sea for a long time.'

❷ 十只鸡蛋
Shí zhī jīdàn

陈太太打电话到楼下的小商店买了
Chén tàitai dǎdiànhuà dào lóuxià de xiǎo shāngdiàn mǎi le

十二只鸡蛋。但是，她看到送来的鸡蛋
shí'èr zhī jīdàn Dànshì tā kàndào sòng lai de jīdàn

只有十只。
zhǐyǒu shí zhī

她打电话给商店的老板。陈太太
Tā dǎdiànhuà gěi shāngdiàn de lǎobǎn Chén tàitai

问："我早上买的不是十二只鸡蛋吗？"
wèn Wǒ zǎoshang mǎi de bù shì shí'èr zhī jīdàn ma

老板说："是啊，有问题吗？"
Lǎobǎn shuō Shì a yǒu wèntí ma

陈太太说："为什么我只收到十只
Chén tàitai shuō Wèishénme wǒ zhǐ shōudào shí zhī

鸡蛋呢？"
jīdàn ne

老板说："是这样的，其中两只鸡蛋
Lǎobǎn shuō Shì zhèyàng de qízhōng liǎng zhī jīdàn

坏了，我们代你丢了。"
huài le wǒmen dài nǐ diū le

Little store at the street

Translation

❷ Ten Eggs

Mrs. Chen phoned the small shop downstairs ordering a dozen eggs.
However, only ten eggs were delivered.

She called the shop owner again asking, 'I ordered a dozen eggs this
morning, as far as I remember.'

The owner replied, 'Yeah, you're right. What's the matter?'

Mrs. Chen said, 'How come I only got ten eggs?'

The owner answered, 'Well, this is what happened. Two of the eggs
were bad. We threw them away for you.'

Mǎi xié
❸ 买鞋

Yī gè nǚrén dào yī
一 个 女人 到 一

jiān shāngdiàn mǎi píxié
间 商店 买 皮鞋。

Tā kàn le yī shuāng
她 看 了 一 双

yòu yī shuāng shì le zhè
又 一 双， 试 了 这

shuāng yòu shì nà shuāng
双 又 试 那 双。

Zuìhòu tā xuǎn chu le
最后， 她 选 出 了

zìjǐ zuì xǐ'ài de yī
自己 最 喜爱 的 一

shuāng xié
双 鞋。

Shoe store

Tā duì fúwùyuán shuō   Qǐng bǎ wǒ zuì zǎo kàn de
她 对 服务员 说："请 把 我 最 早 看 的

nà shuāng xié ná gěi wǒ
那 双 鞋 拿 给 我。"

Fúwùyuán wèn   Shì bu shì huángsè de nà shuāng
服务员 问："是 不 是 黄 色 的 那 双 ？"

Tā shuō   Shì de
她 说："是 的。"

Fúwùyuán shuō   Duìbuqǐ   xiǎojiě   Nà shuāng huángsè
服务员 说："对 不 起, 小 姐。那 双 黄 色

de xié wǒmen zhǐyǒu yī shuāng zài liǎng xiǎoshí qián yǐjīng
的 鞋 我们 只有 一 双 , 在 两 小 时 前 已经

gěi yī gè bǐ nǐ lái de wǎn de kèrén mǎi le
给 一 个 比 你 来 得 晚 的 客人 买 了。"

Translation

❸ Buying Shoes

A woman went to a store to buy shoes.

She browsed the shoes and tried on one pair after another. Finally, she decided which pair of shoes to buy.

She said to the attendant, 'Please bring me the first pair of shoes I tried on at the beginning.'

The attendant said, 'The pair of yellow shoes?'

She answered, 'Yes.'

The attendant said, 'I'm sorry, Madam. We only carry one pair of yellow shoes. A customer who came in later than you bought them two hours ago.'

④ 一 公斤
Yī gōngjīn

一 个 女人 拿 着 一 包
Yī gè nǚrén ná zhe yī bāo

花生 进入 商店。
huāshēng jìnrù shāngdiàn

她 很 生气 地 对 服务员
Tā hěn shēngqì de duì fúwùyuán

A Chinese traditional balance

说:"半 小时 前,我 的 儿子 在 这里 买 了
shuō Bàn xiǎoshí qián wǒ de érzi zài zhèlǐ mǎi le

一 公斤 花生。你 看,才 这么 一点儿,哪 有
yī gōngjīn huāshēng Nǐ kàn cái zhème yīdiǎnr nǎ yǒu

一 公斤 呢?"
yī gōngjīn ne

服务员 说:"太太,这 问题 你 该 问 你
Fúwùyuán shuō Tàitai zhè wèntí nǐ gāi wèn nǐ

的 儿子 吧。"
de érzi ba

Translation

④ One Kilogram

A woman entered a store carrying a bag of peanuts.

She said to the attendant angrily, 'My son bought a kilogram of peanuts from you half an hour ago. Look! How can such a small amount of stuff weigh one kilogram?'

The attendant replied, 'Maybe you should ask your son this question, Madam.'

Bargaining (讲价 , *Jiangjia*)

Nowadays, price tags are attached to all the items carried in supermarkets and retail shops, and customers just have to take their pick. However, some people consider 'bargaining' (讲价) as the spice of life, saying it is so much fun arguing with shopkeepers over the price. Without the haggling, they would feel they are living pretty dull lives. For many buyers, if they can drive a hard bargain with their skills and eloquence, they will get some kind of personal satisfaction out of it in addition to saving money.

An enthusiastic bargain master offers bargaining tips that customers can use to haggle with retailers and avoid wasting hard earned money. For example, stay calm. If you find an item you like, be sure to behave with perfect composure. Moreover, criticize mercilessly. No matter what you have picked, make sure to search studiously to find something wrong with the item. If you really can't find a defect, start picking holes in the item's color or some other minor area, trying to make the retailer feel 'disheartened' so that you can make a sure thing of a lower price . Of course, you should also haggle over the price cold-heartedly and have the courage to go back and try again.

Bargaining can be regarded as a discipline. A true bargain master is probably an amateur psychologist. Nowadays, there are professional bargainers whose job is to help people haggle over the price. These professionals bargain over prices with their knowledge about products and their 'silver tongues', and charge a commission of a certain percentage on the money saved. They don't have a fixed monthly salary, but they can earn up to several thousand Renminbis.

GAMES FOR FUN

In China, in order to avoid false accounting, figures of many invoices and receipts are not written in Arabic numbers but Chinese characters. Do you know the Chinese character numbers below? Give it a try.

(Hint: You can try to read the Chinese words aloud if you can't understand them at all, or perhaps you can picture them.[write them])

(A) 陆佰柒拾捌 (*liu bai qi shi ba*)

(B) 壹仟叁佰伍拾贰 (*yi qian san bai wu shi er*)

(C) 肆万陆仟玖佰壹拾叁 (*si wan liu qian jiu bai yi shi san*)

坐车与开车

Zuòchē yǔ kāichē

Riding and Driving

Pre-reading Questions

1. A good transportation system makes life convenient. Many people prefer driving their own car to taking public transport. How about you?

2. Share one of your memorable experiences about traffic (e.g. helping someone in need, congestion, an accident) with your friends.

---

❶ 老太太和小男孩

Lǎo tàitai hé xiǎo nánhái

一个老太太坐公交车去市场买东西。
Yī gè lǎo tàitai zuò gōngjiāochē qù shìchǎng mǎi dōngxi

她上了公交车后，一个小男孩站
Tā shàng le gōngjiāochē hòu, yī gè xiǎo nánhái zhàn

起来把座位让给她。
qilai bǎ zuòwèi ràng gěi tā

老太太要他坐下去，对他说："我还
Lǎo tàitai yào tā zuò xiaqu duì tā shuō Wǒ hái

很年轻，不需要你把座位让给我。"
hěn niánqīng bù xūyào nǐ bǎ zuòwèi ràng gěi wǒ

72

Guò le yīhuìr
过 了 一 会 儿,

xiǎo nánhái yòu zhàn le
小 男 孩 又 站 了

qǐlái lǎo tàitai yòu yào
起 来, 老 太 太 又 要

tā zuò xiaqu
他 坐 下 去。

In the Chinese bus

Lǎo tàitai shuō Nǐ
老 太 太 说:"你

zhēnde bù yòng bǎ zuòwèi ràng gěi wǒ wǒ méi nàme lǎo
真 的 不 用 把 座 位 让 给 我, 我 没 那 么 老。"

Xiǎo nánhái hǎo jǐ cì zhàn qilai lǎo tàitai dōu yào
小 男 孩 好 几 次 站 起 来, 老 太 太 都 要

tā zuò xiaqu
他 坐 下 去。

Zhōngyú xiǎo nánhái kū le
终 于, 小 男 孩 哭 了。

Tā kū zhe shuō Lǎo tàitai wǒjiā yǐjing guò le
他 哭 着 说:"老 太 太, 我 家 已 经 过 了

hǎo jǐ gè zhàn nǐ wèishénme bù ràng wǒ huíjiā ne
好 几 个 站, 你 为 什 么 不 让 我 回 家 呢?"

Translation

❶ Old Lady and Little Boy

An old lady took a bus to do shopping at the market.

After the lady got on the bus, a little boy stood up to yield his seat to her.

The old lady asked the boy to sit down and said to him, 'I'm still very young. I don't need you to offer me the seat.'

After a while, the little boy stood up again. But the old lady still asked him to sit down.

The old lady said, 'There's really no need for you to yield your seat to me. I'm not that old.'

After that, the little boy stood up several times. Still, the old lady asked him to sit down.

Finally, the little boy cried.

He cried and said, 'Old lady, I've already passed my stop several times. Why didn't you let me get off the bus?'

❷ Zuìhòu yī bān gōngjiāochē
最后 一 班 公交车

Yǒu yī gè nǚhái xiàbān hěn wǎn yào zuò zuìhòu yī
有 一 个 女孩 下班 很 晚，要 坐 最后 一

bān gōngjiāochē huíjiā
班 公交车 回家。

Chinese bus

她在车站等了很久，一直没有等到那一班车。

终于，一辆公交车慢慢地开了过来。

虽然这辆车的车门打开了，但没有在她的面前停下来。

女孩着急了，追上公交车，找了一个座位坐下来。

这时候，她发现车里面一个人都没有，连司机也不在。可是，车还在往前走着。

她想了一想，马上离开了公交车。

当这辆公交车开过她的面前的时候，她看见司机和几个男人正在努力地推着这辆坏了的公交车。

Translation

❷ The Last Bus

A girl got off work very late and needed to take the last bus home.

She waited at the bus station for a long time, but the bus she expected didn't arrive.

At last, the girl saw a bus slowly coming towards her. Although the door was open, the bus did not stop in front of her.

The girl got worried, so she managed to get on the bus and found a seat to sit down.

Just then, she noticed that no one, including the driver, was on the bus. But, the bus still kept running.

The girl thought for a while. Then, she got off the bus immediately.

When the bus slowly passed her, the girl saw the driver and several other guys pushing the broken-down bus with great effort.

❸ 意外

Yìwài

Jīntiān shàngwǔ zài fángzi pángbiān de mǎlùshang chū le

今天 上午, 在 房子 旁边 的 马路上 出 了

jiāotōng yìwài Yī liàng gōngjiāochē zhuàng le yī gè xíngrén

交通 意外。一 辆 公交车 撞 了 一 个 行人。

Xíngrén de jiǎo shòushāng

行人 的 脚 受伤

le

了。

Zhèshíhou jǐngchá

这时候, 警察

hái méiyǒu dào

还 没有 到。

A mobile police post in China

司机 停 了 车，看 了 一 会儿。他 很 生气，
对 行人 说："你 为什么 不 注意 一些 呢？我
是 一 个 很 好 的 司机，开车 十 年 了，从来
没有 出 过 意外！"

行人 听 了 司机 的 话，也 很 生气。他
接 着 说："我 是 一 个 很 好 的 行人。我
走路 已经 四十 多 年 了，也 从来 没有 出 过
意外！"

Translation

❸ Accident

A traffic accident happened on the road next to my house this morning. A bus hit a pedestrian, who got his feet hurt.

While the police were on the way, the driver stopped the bus and gave a quick look. He got angry, shouting to the pedestrian, 'Why didn't you pay more attention? I'm a very good driver. I've been driving for over ten years and I've never had an accident!'

Hearing what the driver said, the pedestrian also got mad. He added, 'I'm a very good pedestrian. For over forty years, I walked to wherever I wanted and have never had an accident!'

The Pain of Congestion

'It is not difficult to buy a car, but it is hard to get where you're going to.' With the economic growth and the continued expansion of cities in China, the 'urban disease' of traffic congestion is rapidly spreading from China's first tier cities to second and third tier cities. Overnight, traffic congestion became a problem faced by all society.

Take Beijing, the capital of China, for example: At peak times of the day when people are traveling to and from work, traffic is generally jammed on city roads, with the saturation flow rate on some lanes reaching up to 95%. The average saturation flow rate during the day is more than 70%, and the vehicle speed also drops to about 10 kilometers per hour, which is the same as that of riding a bicycle. Everyone, whether they are drivers or bus commuters, are complaining, and Beijing's growing traffic congestion is bringing headaches even to the traffic control department.

It is well-known that the world's impression of China used to be 'the bicycle kingdom'. However, this label is used by fewer and fewer people as a description . The rapid growth in the number of cars in China indicates the nation's full fledged entry into a 'car society', which brings along with it a series of conflicts: contributing to the energy shortage, air pollution by emissions, and traffic congestion.

It is extremely urgent that traffic congestion be relieved, so Chinese experts proposed measures such as restricting private cars, making more roads, exerting great efforts to develop public transportation, and enhancing the traffic management level.

One thing is certain: Addressing traffic congestion will be a long, difficult process. .

Traffic jam

GAMES FOR FUN

You are a tourist in Beijing. Due to the serious traffic congestion, you decided to take a subway to your destination.

In the subway station, the only information you can rely on is the Beijing subway map. Beijing has a large subway network with numerous lines. How can you reach the destination with the shortest travelling time? Let's try.

(1) From 圆明园(Yuanmingyuan) to 北京机场(Beijing Capital Airport)

4号线 → ___(a)___ → ___(b)___

(2) From 朝阳门 (Chaoyangmen) to 奥林匹克公园(Olympic Green)

2号线 → ___(c)___ → ___(d)___ → ___(e)___

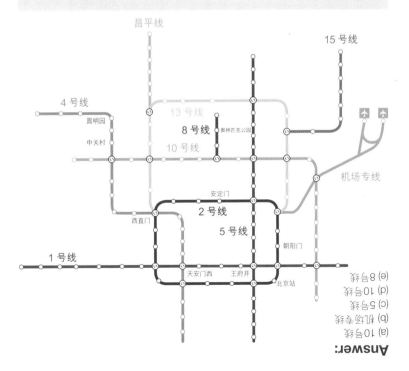

Answer:
(a) 10号线
(b) 机场专线
(c) 5号线
(d) 10号线
(e) 8号线

音乐家与艺术家

Yīnyuèjiā yǔ yìshùjiā

Musician and Artist

Pre-reading Questions

1. Can you name some famous musicians or artists? Share what you know about their stories and what lead to their success.

2. Everybody has his/her own talent. What is yours?

---

❶ Nǚgāoyīn
女高音

Yī gè dǎoyǎn wánchéng le yī
一 个 导 演 完 成 了 一

bù diànyǐng xiǎng wèi tā pèishàng hǎo
部 电 影 , 想 为 它 配 上 好

de yīnyuè
的 音 乐 。

Tā duì yī gè yīnyuèjiā shuō
他 对 一 个 音 乐 家 说 :

Nǐ kànguo wǒ de diànyǐng hòu
"你 看 过 我 的 电 影 后 ,

juéde zěnyàng
觉 得 怎 样 ? "

Soprano

80

Yīnyuèjiā shuō Gùshi hěn pǔtōng yǎnyuán yě shuō
音乐家 说："故事 很 普通, 演员 也 说

de tài duō le
得 太 多 了。"

Dǎoyǎn shuō Xièxie nǐ de yìjiàn Nǐ rènwéi
导演 说："谢谢 你 的 意见。你 认为

shénme yīnyuè shìhé zhè bù diànyǐng ne
什么 音乐 适合 这 部 电影 呢?"

Yīnyuèjiā shuō Yīnyuè bù zhòngyào zuì zhòngyào
音乐家 说："音乐 不 重要, 最 重要

shì diànyǐng kuàiyào jiéshù de shíhou yào yǒu nǚgāoyīn de
是 电影 快要 结束 的 时候,要 有 女高音 的

biǎoyǎn
表演。"

Dǎoyǎn shuō Wèishénme ne
导演 说："为什么 呢?"

Yīnyuèjiā shuō Bù zhèyàng zuò guānzhòng hái zài
音乐家 说："不 这样 做, 观众 还 在

shuìjiào bù dǒngde líkāi
睡觉, 不 懂得 离开。"

Translation

1 Soprano

A director made a film and wanted to have good background music edited into it.

The director asked a musician, 'What do you think of my film after viewing it?'

The musician answered, 'The plot is ordinary, and the performers talk too much.'

The director said, 'Thank you for giving me your opinion. What kind of music do you think fits this film?'

The musician replied, 'Music is not that important. What matters is we need a soprano who performs near the end of the film.'

The director asked, 'Why?'

The musician said, 'Without doing that, the viewers would stay asleep, not knowing it's time to leave.'

❷ 喜欢
Xǐhuan

Playing Piano

一 个 音乐 家 很 高兴 地 对 朋友 说：“昨天 晚上，
Yī gè yīnyuèjiā hěn gāoxìng de duì péngyou shuō Zuótiān wǎnshang

我 在 家里 弹 钢琴 的 时候，有人 用 石头 打破 了 我家 的 窗子。”
wǒ zài jiāli tán gāngqín de shíhou yǒurén yòng shítou dǎpò le wǒjiā de chuāngzi

朋友 说：“这个 人 一定 很 不 喜欢 听 你 的 音乐 了。”
Péngyou shuō Zhège rén yīdìng hěn bù xǐhuan tīng nǐ de yīnyuè le

音乐家 说：“不 是 的。他 太 喜欢 听 了，所以 打破 窗子，他 好 听 得 更 清楚 一些。”
Yīnyuèjiā shuō Bù shì de Tā tài xǐhuan tīng le suǒyǐ dǎpò chuāngzi tā hǎo tīng de gèng qīngchu yīxiē

Translation

❷ Enjoying Music

A musician said happily to a friend of his, 'A guy broke the window of my house with a stone while I was playing the piano last night.'

His friend said, 'This guy surely didn't like the music you were playing.'

The musician replied, 'You're wrong. He liked it so much that he broke the window to listen to the music more clearly.'

Yìwài
❸ 意外

Yǒu yī gè rén tā bù dǒngde huàhuà dàn hěn xǐhuan
有一个人，他不懂得画画，但很喜欢

tí yìjiàn
提意见。

Yǒu yī cì tā láidào yī gè huàjiā de jiāzhōng
有一次，他来到一个画家的家中，

kàndào zhuōzishang fàng le yī zhāng gānggāng wánchéng de huà
看到桌子上放了一张刚刚完成的画。

Zhè zhāng huà hěn jiǎndān zhǐyǒu yī gè hóngsè de yòu
这张画很简单，只有一个红色的又

yuán yòu dà de dōngxi
圆又大的东西。

Tā duì huàjiā shuō Zhè huà huà de tài hǎo le
他对画家说："这画画得太好了，

wǒ hěn xǐhuan
我很喜欢。"

Huàjiā tīng le hěn gāoxìng shuō Nǐ néng gàosu
画家听了很高兴，说："你能告诉

wǒ nǐ xǐhuan zhè zhāng huà de yuányīn ma
我，你喜欢这张画的原因吗？"

Zhège rén shuō Tā ràng wǒ hěn xiǎng chī dōngxi
这个人说："它让我很想吃东西。
Nǐ bǎ yī zhī shú de jīdàn huà zài huàshang zhēn ràng rén
你把一只熟的鸡蛋画在画上，真让人
gǎndào yìwài a
感到意外啊。"
Huàjiā tīng le zhīhòu méiyǒu shuōhuà
画家听了之后，没有说话。
Zhège rén hěn yǒu xìnxīn de shuō Zhème hǎo de huà
这个人很有信心地说："这么好的画
yīdìng yǒu yī gè tèbié de míngzi Nǐ néng gàosu wǒ ma
一定有一个特别的名字。你能告诉我吗？"
Huàjiā shuō Tā jiàozuò Zǎoshang de tàiyáng
画家说："它叫做《早上的太阳》。"

Translation

❸ Unexpected

A man didn't know how to paint, but he liked to give his opinions.

One day, he visited a painter and saw on the table a painting that was just finished.

The painting was very simple. It was only a red blob that was big and round.

He said to the painter, 'This painting is excellent. I like it very much.'

Feeling happy to hear what he said, the painter asked, 'Could you tell me why you like it?'

The man replied, 'It makes me feel hungry. You painted a cooked egg. What a surprise!'

After hearing this, the painter did not say anything.

Then, the man asked confidently, 'You must have given a special title to such an excellent painting. Could you tell me what it is titled?'

The painter answered, 'It's called "The Sun in the Morning".'

The Making of an Artist

In China, there was a painter whose fine works today are worthy of being handed down to future generations. Although he was not prolific, on domestic and overseas art markets his paintings were sold again and again for high auction prices of several million dollars or up to ten million yuan, with the total transaction value reaching more than one billion dollars. He donated most of his money to society and lived in a small house of twenty or thirty square meters.

The painting of Wu Guanzhong

This respected painter was Wu Guanzhong.

Wu Guanzhong was a phenomenon in China's art circle. Exactly how much popularity did his paintings enjoy? In 1987, Hong Kong organized 'the retrospective exhibition of Wu Guanzhong's works', and all of the over one hundred works exhibited were sold within 40 minutes. In 2007, his painting 'The Jiaohe Ruins' fetched over forty million yuan, an astronomical price that was the highest figure paid at auction for a piece by a living mainland artist at that time.

Wu Guanzhong was renowned around the world for his artistic achievements, but he was always very humble. He used to say, 'I disappoint my expectations of painting (我负丹青, *Wofudanqing*).' He used the word 'disappoint' (负) to show he would never be satisfied in pursuing artistic achievement. Moreover, he was in the habit of 'destroying his paintings' for many years. If he was slightly dissatisfied with his painting, he would destroy it personally without hesitation, even though the painting had been finished and mounted. Someone said that Wu Guanzhong burned down a luxury house every time he destroyed a painting. However, he never changed the habit of 'painting till he dies and destroying his works along the way.'

GAMES FOR FUN

Below is a work of Chinese calligraphy. The calligrapher combined four Chinese words into one character. Do you know which four words they are?

Answer:
"招财进宝" (*zhaocaijinbao*), means "to bring in money and treasures".

Jiā yǔ jiǎn

加与减

Addition and Subtraction

Pre-reading Questions

1. Life is full of Mathematics. For example, we do simple Math during buying and selling transactions, while weather forecasting requires highly accurate calculations. Can you give more examples that involve Math?

2. In Chinese, there are at least two ways to write numbers. How many ways can you write/recognize? (Hint: An example can be found in chapter 9.)

Wèn wèntí

❶ 问 问题

Dìdi wèn wǒ   Liǎng gè píngguǒ duōshao qián

弟弟 问 我："两 个 苹果 多少 钱？"

Wǒ shuō   Sān yuán

我 说："三 元。"

Dìdi yòu wèn   Wǔ tiáo xiāngjiāo duōshao qián

弟弟 又 问："五 条 香蕉 多少 钱？"

Wǒ shuō   Sì yuán   Zěnme le   yǒu wèntí ma

我 说："四 元。怎么 了，有 问题 吗？"

Selling fruits

Dìdi hái zài wèn
弟弟还在问："两个苹果和五条
Liǎng gè píngguǒ hé wǔ tiáo

xiāngjiāo duōshao qián
香蕉多少钱？"

Wǒ bù míngbai dìdi wèishénme wèn zhèxiē shìqing
我不明白弟弟为什么问这些事情。

Wǒ xiǎng le yīhuìr wèn dìdi Bù shì qī yuán
我想了一会儿，问弟弟："不是七元

ma
吗？"

Dìdi shuō Xièxie nǐ
弟弟说："谢谢你。"

Wǒ wèn Wèishénme
我问："为什么？"

Dìdi shuō Zhè shì jīntiān de gōngkè
弟弟说："这是今天的功课。"

Translation

❶ Asking Questions

My younger brother asked me, 'How much do two apples cost?'

I answered, 'Three dollars.'

He asked again, 'How much do five bananas cost?'

I answered, 'Four dollars. What's the matter? Anything wrong?'

Still, my brother asked me, 'How much do two apples and five bananas cost?'

I had no idea why my brother asked me these questions.

I thought for a while and then answered my brother, 'Seven dollars. Am I right?'

He replied, 'Thank you.'

I asked, 'Why?'

He said, 'I'm now doing my homework for today.'

Fángjiān
❷ 房间

Lǐ xiānsheng gāng cóng Xiānggǎng lǚyóu huílai
李 先生 刚 从 香港 旅游 回来。

Tā duì wǒ shuō Xiānggǎng jiǔdiàn fángjiān de
他 对 我 说:"香港 酒店 房间 的

fèiyong tài gāo le měitiān yào yuán Wǒ zhù le yī
费用 太 高 了,每天 要 1000 元。我 住 了 一

xīngqī huā le yuán
星期,花 了 7000 元。"

Wǒ diǎntóu biǎoshì tóngyì shuō yuán zhēnde
我 点头 表示 同意,说:"7000 元,真的

tài gāo le
太 高 了。"

Lǐ xiānsheng shuō　　Shì a
李 先生 说："是 啊！"

Wǒ shuō　　Nǐ zài Xiānggǎng yī xīngqī　gāi dào guo
我 说："你 在 香港 一 星期，该 到 过

hěnduō hǎo dìfang　mǎi le hěnduō hǎo dōngxi huílai ba
很多 好 地方，买 了 很多 好 东西 回来 吧。"

Lǐ xiānsheng shuō　　Hǎo dìfang　Hǎo dōngxi
李 先生 说："好 地方？好 东西？"

Wǒ hěn qíguài　wèn　　Yǒu wèntí ma
我 很 奇怪，问："有 问题 吗？"

Lǐ xiānsheng shuō　　Wǒ shénme dìfang dōu méiyǒu qù
李 先生 说："我 什么 地方 都 没有 去，

shénme dōngxi dōu méiyǒu mǎi
什么 东西 都 没有 买。"

Wǒ wèn　　Wèishénme ne
我 问："为什么 呢？"

Lǐ xiānsheng shuō　　Wǒ jiāo le　　　yuán zěnme
李 先生 说："我 交 了 7000 元，怎么

kěyǐ ràng fángjiān kòng zhe ne
可以 让 房间 空 着 呢？"

Peninsula hotel in HongKong

90

Translation

❷ The Room

Mr. Lee has just come back from his trip to Hong Kong.

He said to me, 'They charge too much for hotel rooms in Hong Kong. It cost me 1000 dollars per day. I lived there for one week, and I spent 7000 dollars.'

I nodded to give my agreement, saying, '7000 dollars. That was way too much.'

Mr. Lee said, 'Tell me about it!'

I asked, 'Since you stayed in Hong Kong for one week, you must have been to many places and bought a lot of good stuff.

Mr. Lee replied, 'Good places? Good stuff?'

I felt curious, so I asked, 'Did I say something wrong?'

Mr. Lee answered, 'I didn't go anyplace, and I didn't buy anything.'

I asked, 'How come?'

Mr. Lee said, 'I spent 7000 dollars. How could I leave the room unoccupied?'

❸ 100 分

考试 成绩 出来 了。

小 王 回到 家里，说：“英语 和 数学 考 了 100 分。”

爸爸 妈妈 听 后 很 高兴。

小 王 接着 说：“是 加 起来 100 分。”

Bàba tīng le hěn shēngqì bù ràng tā chīfàn
爸爸 听 了 很 生气, 不 让 他 吃饭。

Māma bù tóngyì shuō fēn yě bùcuò le
妈妈 不 同意, 说："100 分 也 不 错 了。

Yī gè fēn yī gè fēn zǒngyǒu yī gè shì hégé
一 个 40 分, 一 个 60 分, 总有 一 个 是 合格

de
的。"

Xiǎo Wáng dī zhe tóu xiǎoshēng shuō Mā bù shì
小 王 低 着 头, 小声 说："妈, 不 是

zhèyàng de Yīngyǔ shì fēn shùxué shì fēn jiā
这样 的。英语 是 10 分, 数学 是 0 分, 加

qilai fēn
起来 100 分。"

Translation

❸ 100 Points

The test score was announced.

Xiao Wang returned home and he said, 'I got 100 points for English and mathematics tests.'

His parents were delighted to learn about it.

Xiao Wang added, 'I'm talking about the combined points.'

His father got very angry after hearing this, so he did not allow Xiao Wang to have dinner.

His mother tried to smooth things over by saying, 'It is not bad to get 100 points. 40 points for one test and 60 points for the other, he must have passed one of them.'

Xiao Wang whispered with his head hanging down, 'Mom, it's not what you think. I got 10 points for English and 0 points for mathematics. So combined they are 100 points.'

Wǎng hòu tuì
❹ 往 后 退

Zài gōnglùshang yī liàng chūzūchē tíng le xiàlái
在 公路上， 一 辆 出租车 停 了 下来。

Xiānsheng nǐ yào qù de dìfang dào le Chēfèi shì
"先生， 你 要 去 的 地方 到 了。 车费 是

yuán
22 元。"

Ā duìbuqǐ Qǐng nǐ wǎng hòu tuì yīdiǎnr hǎo
"啊， 对不起。 请 你 往 后 退 一点儿 好

ma
吗？"

Wèishénme ne
"为什么 呢？"

Wǒ shēnshang zhǐyǒu yuán
"我 身上 只有 20 元。"

Translation

❹ Going Back

A taxi stopped on the road.

'Sir, this is it. The fare is 22 dollars.'

'Oh, I'm sorry. Could you please go back a little bit?'

'Why are you asking me to do that?'

'Because I've only got 20 dollars.'

Chinese Attitudes Towards Money

There are many people dreaming about making a fortune in China. Therefore, at the start of the New Year, people greet each other most of the time by saying 'I wish you happiness and prosperity. (恭喜发财 , *gongxifacai*)'. Many people even paste red paper couplets to the door with these four Chinese characters 'I wish you happiness and prosperity. (恭喜发财)' in order to bring good luck. Also, people generally prepare whole fish dishes at parties, where they are entertaining guests at banquets or family get-togethers. This represents the hope that guests live in abundance year after year, namely 'be blessed with (or have) abundance every year (年年有余 , *niannianyouyu*)'. 'Fish (鱼 , *yu*)' and 'abundance (余 , *yu*)' are pronounced the same way in Chinese.

Chinese people are very cautious about money. While conducting financial transactions, they generally try to hand over the money and receive the goods simultaneously, and they usually check the receipt on the spot, never doing things like Koreans who tend to delay solving issues. If Chinese people are withdrawing money from the bank, you may often see them counting bank notes one by one. They don't even seem to trust the counting machine.

Moreover, the Chinese like to save money, and they have had this habit for a long time. Whenever they get money, the first thing they do is save it, even though they will likely need to spend money the following day. With the economic development of the past few years, however, a wave of consumption is hitting the younger generation in China. Even so, saving money is still the main trend. The reason why the Chinese save money is to prepare for life in retirement and medical care in the future.

Chinese New Year decoration (挥春 , *huichun*) with auspicious greetings

Moreover, Chinese people like to make investments. The items they invest in are mainly property and antiques, because many people think that the profits gained from investment in property far outweigh the risks involved, and antiques have become a more and more popular form of investment in recent years. It is estimated that there are currently around 70 million antique enthusiasts in China.

GAMES FOR FUN

This is an IQ question about fares, can you solve the question?

A and B ride on a carriage heading in the same direction. A gets down after 4 miles, and then B gets down after another 4 miles. The total fare is $12, how much should A and B pay respectively?

Answer:

The total fare is $12, both A and B ride on the carriage for 4 miles, so the fare for the first 4 miles should be $6, hence, the fare for A is $3. B should pay $3 for the first 4 miles, and $6 for the last 4 miles which he rides alone, so his total fare should be $9.

Only in this way the share is fair.

The formulas are:

The fare of A: $12 \times [4/(4+4)] \div 2 = 3$

The fare of B: $(12 \times 4/(4+4) \div 2) + 12 \times 4/(4+4) = 9$

Glossary

GCS: HanBan / Confucius Institute Headquaters, The Graded Chinese Syllables, Characters and Words for the Application of Teaching Chinese to the Speakers of Other Languages, 2010.

shí tou	石头	stone	1	*82*
diū	丢	throw away	2	*19*
jiāo tōng	交通	traffic	1	*76*
guāng míng	光明	shine, brightness	1	*25*
guān xīn	关心	show consideration	1	*20*
hé gé	合格	pass	1	*92*
tóng shì	同事	colleague	1	*19*
dì zhǐ	地址	address	2	*44*
zì diǎn	字典	dictionary	1	*36*
nián qīng	年轻	young	1	*16*
chéng jì	成绩	score, result	1	*3*
lǎo bǎn	老板	boss	1	*40*
kǎo shì	考试	test, examination	1	*34*
xíngrén	行人	pedestrian	1	*76*
zuò wén	作文	composition	1	*1*
kùn nan	困难	difficult	1	*3*
shēng yīn	声音	sound	1	*11*
hù shi	护士	nurse	1	*17*
bào zhǐ	报纸	newspaper	1	*42*
tiáo jiàn	条件	condition	1	*41*
dù zi	肚子	stomach	2	*48*
shòu shāng	受伤	hurt	1	*76*
wèi dao	味道	taste	1	*62*
qí guài	奇怪	strange	1	*9*
hū rán	忽然	unexpectedly	1	*59*
fàng xīn	放心	relax	1	*43*

fú wù yuán	服务员	attendant, waiter	1	*57*
bēi zi	杯子	cup	1	*60*
zhù yì	注意	pay attention	1	*77*
zhī shi	知识	knowledge	1	*6*
jīng guò	经过	pass by	1	*29*
huā	花	spend	1	*89*
huā shēng	花生	peanuts	2	*69*
biǎo yǎn	表演	performance	1	*81*
gù shi	故事	plot, story	1	*81*
diǎn tóu	点头	nod	1	*89*
xiāng xìn	相信	believe	1	*27*
tū rán	突然	suddenly	1	*9*
píng guǒ	苹果	apple	2	*87*
gāng qín	钢琴	piano	2	*82*
yīn yuè	音乐	music	1	*80*
shí wù	食物	food	1	*57*
xiāng jiāo	香蕉	banana	2	*87*
zhǔn bèi	准备	wait for, prepare	1	*51*
yuán yīn	原因	reason	1	*83*
kū	哭	cry, weep	1	*26*
hài pà	害怕	afraid, fear, worried	1	*4*
róng yì	容易	easy	1	*54*
chà	差	bad, lousy	1	*33*
lǚ yóu	旅游	travel	1	*89*
xiāo xi	消息	information	1	*42*
tè bié	特别	special	1	*84*

téng	疼	pain	1	*48*
gǎn jǐn	赶紧	hurry	1	*19*
sòng	送	give as a present	1	*19*
shì hé	适合	fit, suit	1	*2*
shāng diàn	商店	store, shop	1	*66*
shāng liang	商量	discuss	1	*22*
jiào shì	教室	classroom	1	*38*
qīng chu	清楚	clear	1	*35*
lǐ yóu	理由	reason, excuse	1	*53*
lí kāi	离开	away from, leave	1	*13*
dàn gāo	蛋糕	cake	2	*61*
wēn nuǎn	温暖	warm	1	*25*
yào	药	medicine	1	*49*
yì jiàn	意见	opinion, comment	1	*42*
yì wài	意外	accident	1	*53*
xīn wén	新闻	news	1	*65*
zhào piàn	照片	photograph	1	*21*
zhào gù	照顾	take care	1	*9*
yǎn yuán	演员	performers	1	*81*
shuì jiào	睡觉	sleep	1	*10*
xū yào	需要	need	1	*17*
zēng jiā	增加	increase	1	*41*
zhuàng	撞	hit, crash	2	*76*
xié	鞋	shoes	1	*19*
dǒng	懂	understand	1	*33*
jǐng chá	警察	police	1	*76*

dǎo yǎn	导演	director	1	*80*
tài du	态度	attitude	1	*38*
ài qíng	爱情	love	1	*27*
jiǎn dān	简单	simple	1	*51*
jǐn zhāng	紧张	nervous	1	*13*
liàn xí	练习	practice	1	*6*
zhōng yú	终于	finally	1	*28*
jié shù	结束	end, finish	1	*81*
guān zhòng	观众	viewer, audience	1	*81*
guī dìng	规定	rule	1	*53*
tǎo lùn	讨论	discuss	1	*27*
shuō huà	说话	speak	1	*6*
fù zé	负责	responsible of	1	*42*
fèi yong	费用	fee	1	*89*
qián	钱	money	1	*14*
qiān bǐ	铅笔	pencil	2	*35*
wèn tí	问题	question	1	*66*
wén	闻	smell	1	*64*
gù kè	顾客	customer	1	*45*
jiāo ào	骄傲	proud of	2	*12*